"With *Tones Of Home* Thomas A. Erb takes us home for some deeply disturbing holidays. Chilling and full of bizarre twists. Thumbs up." – Jonathan Maberry, New York Times best-selling author of *Flesh & Bone* and *V-Wars*

"Thomas Erb's *Tones Of Home* has to be the bloodiest, the most ruthless, and yet the most honest love story I've come across since Natural Born Killers. Erb put his hooks into me with this one and had me guessing right up to the last page. It's a nail-biter through and through, and I'm betting it's going to leave you as stunned as it left me. Oh-and Quentin Tarantino, if you're looking for your next movie, the search stops here. – Joe McKinney, Bram Stoker Award-winning author of *Inheritance* and *Dead City*

"In *'Tones of Home'* Thomas A. Erb will gently take you by the hand and lead you away from safety. His clean, unpretentious writing style is a treat for any reader. Recommended!" – James Roy Daley - author of *The Dead Parade* and *Terror Town.*

"This one has that wonderful nightmare quality - the one where you know you're dreaming but can't wake up, and imagined terrors are suddenly all too real. In other words, a reader's high." – David Dunwoody. author of *The Harvest Cycle*

"If you're into old school Rock and Roll and like your horror fiction dark and super nasty like I do, you're going to LOVE Thomas A. Erb's new book. *Tones Of Home* is extreme horror at its best and it knocked me on my ass when I read it. Highly recommended!" – Gord Rollo, author of *The Jigsaw Man* and *The Crucifixion Experiments*

'Tones of Home' starts at full-speed and never lets up. Unpredictable and astonishingly bloody! Thomas A. Erb's story telling is a brutal, fast-paced read which hooks the reader in from the very start. Gallons of blood, plenty of violence, and the Fab Four… you'll not have read anything like this before!" – David Moody, author of *Hater* and *Autumn* Series.

For Mom & Dad,

Helter Skelter!

TONES OF HOME

THOMAS A. ERB

COPYRIGHT © 2012 THOMAS A. ERB

This Edition Published 2013 by Crowded
Quarantine Publications
The moral right of the author has been asserted

A CIP catalogue record for this book
is available from the British Library

ISBN 978-0-9576480-0-5

Printed and bound in Great Britain
Crowded Quarantine Publications
34 Cheviot Road
Wolverhampton
West Midlands
WV2 2HD

ACKNOWLEDGEMENTS

When I sat down to write this, I was a bit overwhelmed. After all, anyone who's ever completed a project such as this knows, there is a list a gazillion miles long of amazing people that help make it possible. This novella you're holding in your hands is no different.

My Mom deserves a huge thank you for encouraging me to explore my imagination, no matter where it may lead. (after all, wasn't that the fun part?) That, and her love for reading and Stephen King.

The Beatles. 'Nuff Said. Read on...you will understand.

The following folks are not only amazing writers, they're also my mentors and friends. Now some may not know that they've been serving in such a capacity, but they have. They've generously given me inspiration, guidance, support and encouragement. I hope I'm doing okay.

Jonathan Maberry, Joe McKinney, David Moody, Michael Knost, Brian Keene, Gord Rollo, Rick Hautala

While the writer's life by its very nature is a solitary pursuit, no one can survive on their own. I've been blessed with some incredibly loyal, supportive and brutally honest close friends and fellow writers, beta-readers. Here's a list of such comrades in arms. (I'm sure I've forgotten someone. For that, I'm sorry, I'll make it up to you. Promise.)

Sheldon S. Higdon, Ty Schwamberger, Dean Harrison, David Dunwoody, Kurt Criscione, Gregory Hall Skip Novak, Tim Deal, Danny Evarts, Mark Wholley, Zjonny Morse, Scott Christian Carr, Joseph Mulak, Brady Allen, Andrew Wolter, Charles Day, James Roy Daley, Nick Cato, Steven Shrewsbury, Dave Brockie, Lucy Snyder, Gary Braunbeck, Lawrence C. Connelly, Louise Bohmer, Kevin Lucia, Myr Davies, R. Scott McCoy, Tonia Brown, Adam Millard.

Bridget Manns, Eric Ralston, Cassondria Sergent, Robin Cragg-Cassella, Bruce Cramer, Stacy Gonzalez

Thank you so much for all your time and continuing support. There's much more to come!

For my wife, Shelly.
You make all things possible

Life is what happens while you are busy making other plans.
- John Lennon

I don't believe in killing whatever the reason!
- John Lennon

It was that kind of a crazy afternoon, terrifically cold, and no sun out or anything, and you felt like you were disappearing every time you crossed a road.
- J.D. Salinger, The Catcher in the Rye

Rock and roll music, if you like it, if you feel it, you can't help but move to it. That's what happens to me. I can't help it.
- Elvis Presley

Truth is like the sun. You can shut it out for a time, but it ain't goin' away.
- Elvis Presley

1.

"Till there was you."

"I'm not so sure about this, Ash?" Maurice Ware said as he stared into the snowy night outside the passenger side window. He wrung his hands and could feel his chest tighten. A green sign with white letters appeared out of the night and read: *Sterling Point 21 Miles, Geneva 14 Miles, Arcadia Falls 10 Miles* and at the bottom, in faded print, *Miller Falls 5 Miles.* He felt his pulse quicken and a lump the size of a tennis ball grew in his throat.

"Ah, come on now honey, you're not getting cold feet already, are you?" Ashley Vanslycke teased as she squinted out the snow-covered windshield of the late model Hyundai. He could sense she was smiling and always loved the way her blonde hair fell over her right eye, almost hiding it completely.

"No, of course not babe, it's just . . . I've never met your parents before, let alone your entire family and friends," he admitted and let out a laugh.

"Oh, they're gonna just love you." She leaned over quickly and kissed him. Her tongue darted into his mouth, lost in his dark lips.

"Uh…just keep your eyes on the road would you?" He gently pushed her away and chuckled.

"Ah, how could they not? Look at that cute little face." She cooed and pinched his ebony-colored cheek and gave him a wink.

"Okay, I hope so."

"Well, I love you and that's all that matters, right?" She cocked an eyebrow and gave him a smirk. It did little to ease his queasy stomach and sweaty hands. However, her almond shaped brown eyes had the ability to warm and center him. However, this time, it was a completely different world he was walking into. He rang his clammy hands tighter.

The drumming of the windshield wipers did little to keep the snow away as they drove along the deserted Route 31. The snow hadn't let up since they left the Interstate and headed north toward the town of Miller Falls. The road had been getting snow-covered and more treacherous and Maurice wasn't used to the backwoods roads of New York.

"You okay city boy?" she teased and blew him a kiss. She reached down and turned up the volume on the CD player and Taylor Swift came pining out of the speakers crying, 'Our Song.' He just shook his head.

"How can you listen to that crap?" he asked with a wry smile.

"It's good music babe. Sorry if it's not your fancy schmancy Miles Duffiss," she laughed.

"Davis. It's Miles *DAVIS*, you should know that by now," he retorted and laughed, grabbed her thigh and gave it a gentle squeeze.

"Can we please play something — *anything* — else?" he pleaded, reaching for the eject button on the CD player. She playfully smacked his hand away.

"I guess so, but you owe me Mo." Her eyes and facial expression told him exactly the price that would have to be paid. He didn't mind. He never did.

"Ah, excellent! I have just the thing to mellow me out," he said and grabbed a CD from the sun visor above him.

The lilting opening piano notes and a soft bass floated through the car's interior and the blissful sound raised his spirits immediately. *So what* was always one of his favorite Miles Davis tunes. It took him to a good place. He was happy now. She feigned protest, but he had gotten her into Miles and he always loved the way she danced and moved her beautiful body to the syncopated grooves. He was neck-deep in love with her. He knew it from the first time they met at Nazareth College in Rochester and again during the required Child Abuse Workshop last summer. He was studying to be a music teacher and she was on her way to be an art teacher. He loved her deeply. He'd never felt love so complete and without doubt before. Maybe his mother, but that was different. Ashley was the perfect soul-mate. He stared at her and couldn't believe she actually said yes. The ring, while small, still caught the bluish light from the dash lights and sparkled, making him smile wide.

They were polar opposites on the surface and every other way. Her with her long, flowing blonde hair and enrapturing brown eyes that stole his heart and soul the minute he gazed into them. Her alabaster skin was almost like porcelain. It reminded him of the China dolls his grandma Arlene used to have on her shelves in her living room. It was made even brighter when she was next to his almost jet-black skin tone. She was so outgoing and hyperactive. While he would prefer to stay in her dorm room and watch old *West Wing* or *NCIS* reruns. She was always the one who would drag him out to the club to dance and drink. He preferred the shadow instead of the multi-colored, throbbing lights of the Rochester club scene. She was the one to dance on top of a table, while he stood hiding his face in the darkness. They were never dark enough for him. Nevertheless, he would do anything for her. And she knew it. He never thought he would fall in love with a white girl; it wasn't that he didn't find them attractive; it was more of where he came from. The family back in Pittsboro wouldn't approve. Things are different back home. He was already the first in the family to go to college and for him to leave home and come to New York, was a slap in his father's face. He needed to put some distance between himself and his father. A sudden cold chill overtook him, causing him to shiver.

"Still not used to these upstate New York winters huh Mo?" Ashley chided and turned up the heat.

"Ah, it is what it is, Ash, but you can keep me

warm." He smiled and grabbed her hand and pulled it off the steering wheel and gave it a kiss. He caught her blushing.

They both jumped as Sugarland's *"Baby Girl"* ringtone shattered their loving moment.

She snatched the cell phone from the center console and answered. Maurice grew more nervous as the snow pelted the car and the wind sent white drifts in their path.

"Hello Daddy." Ashley's voice took on a little girl tone and she shot Maurice a sidelong glance.

He gulped not knowing which freaked him out more — her talking on the phone while driving through a snowstorm or the sound of his soon-to-be father-in-law's deep voice on the phone. He couldn't hear specific words, just the low tenor of his speech. That was all he needed to hear.

Growing up in the sticks of North Carolina, he had experienced his share of racism and bigotry. He had heard tales of Wayne County and they came rushing back as they passed a sign that read, *Welcome to Wayne County.* Apparently, rednecks and racist pricks weren't only indigenous to the south. His friend Joe Ward, back at college, warned him of the backwoods mentality some people in Wayne

County had towards blacks and the fact that he was engaged to a pasty white girl didn't help matters any. He didn't know much about her, or her family. All he knew about the Vanslycke family was that they were potato farmers and had tons of relatives in the area. All that aside, he did know that he loved her deeply and she was going to be his bride. The thought sent shivers all over his body and a wide smile broke across his face. He'd never been this happy. Every time he looked at her, he fought to catch his breath. This time was no different.

"Mo, you are gonna so love my *FAM*, I guarantee it," Ashley beamed from underneath her knitted cap. The shaggy tan ball bounced against her face as she boogied to the music. She shot him a wink and her eyes grew wide.

"Ah . . . we're here babe." She was almost shouting as she pointed toward the large sign offering the only light that could be seen in the shock white of the December snowstorm. Maurice looked out the passenger side window and tried to read the old tow-behind, light up sign. Monday Night Football wings and drafts ½ prices. Thursday night Dart league, Christmas Eve — Live Music - *Mo' Whiskey and the Shanty Town Revelers.* "Oh this should be just perfect," he muttered.

"What's that babe?" she asked as she pulled the car slowly off the road and began looking for a parking spot in the packed bar parking lot.

"Oh, uh, that spot over there next to the big Chevy with the humongous tires should be perfect," he quickly quibbled. *Well, it is what it is Mo, you love her, so suck it up bro,* he thought. He was amazed at the number of mammoth-sized trucks in the snow-covered lot. He could hear the twangy sounds of country music booming from inside the roadside bar.

A large layer of snow covered the low sloping roof of the one-storey building. It looked more like a poor man's ski lodge than a Podunk bar. It had a large picture window facing the road and was filled with a large Genesee Cream Ale neon sign sending green and red light splintering the quarter-sized snowflakes that were pelting all outside and burying the patrons 4X4s. A large shoddily built deck, made of obviously used wood, jutted out from the side and broke the parking lot in half. A gaggle of rowdy smokers could be seen on the deck. Maurice and Ashley parked and got out of the car, and looked about the parking lot. An old white Chevy van pulled in behind them and headed down back toward the volleyball court. It left deep trenches of tire tracks as it disappeared behind the building into the snowy night.

"There's no way in hell I'd park down back. This time of year, unless you have four-wheel drive, boy are they screwed." Ashley laughed and turned the car off and gave Maurice a quick smooch and wrapped her knitted scarf around her face and got out. Maurice wasn't relishing the thought of getting out in the cold storm, but *it is what it is*, he told himself and pulled the hood up on his jacket and zipped it up to his nose and forced the door open, fighting against the strong wind blowing in from the north.

The entrance was a simple wooden door with an *Open* sign hung off-kilter, and offered a slight beacon of welcome. The wood was well worn and had the stains of many years embedded in its deep grains. The tall, roughly-poured cement steps that led into the bar were covered in deep, powdery fluff.

"Huh, no footprints," Maurice said.

"Ha, yeah, I'm sure the boys have been here a long while babe," Ashley chuckled. She paused in front of the nearly covered step.

"You ready Mo?" She winked and hugged him and gave him a tight kiss.

"Cut that shit out, or get a goddamn room," a booming voice punched through the howling winds.

Maurice's heart stopped and his breath froze in the freezing night air.

2.

"Oh Darling"

Awall of snow rushed across the packed parking lot and washed over Maurice and Ashley, leaving them covered in freezing snow. All that could be heard was Ashley laughing. Maurice didn't even want to look at the source of the comment. His chest squeezed tight.

Before them, beside the open door, was a monster of a man dressed in stained, dark brown *Carhartt* bib overalls and wearing what looked like a dead raccoon on his head. His long black beard reached his chest and seemed to be matted with a sticky liquid. His lower lip bulged as he smiled. Chewing tobacco, Maurice surmised, and that would explain the nasty beard, he finished.

"'Bout time you got yur ass here, Ash, we've been waiting and ya know Big Daddy don't like waitin'." The burly man looked down at Maurice and gave him a nod and a wink.

"You must be Moooooorice?" He smiled and a long brown tendril of spit escaped from his broken-toothed smile and slithered down until it was lost in the tangled mess of his beard. The man-bear looked Maurice up and down and smiled.

"Uh, yes, I am. Nice to meet you, uhm?" Maurice stuck out his hand and the big man ignored it.

"Do you mind if we come inside, Butch?" Ashley asked, still laughing slightly as she pushed him. He laughed and shifted slightly closer to the door and waved his right hand in a gesture of entrance.

"Sure, come on in," Butch bellowed and watched Maurice as he was forced to squeeze through the small entrance, due to the fact the big man took up most of the doorway.

"Come on in, get warm and have a drink. Dad's buying." Butch smiled; more foul smelling liquid drained from the open spot in his brown and yellow teeth. Maurice felt the man's big belly jut out as he squeezed through and could smell his foul breath as the man laughed. Maurice smiled and held his breath as he finally entered the packed bar. Then he wished he could have his breath back.

If he thought it was white outside, the great snowstorm had nothing on the wall-to-wall all white occupants of the Torchlight Inn. It looks like the cast of Leave it to Beaver and The Andy Griffith Show had a freakish, redneck love child. The bar was filled with laughing, dancing people of all shapes and sizes. All seemed to be fond of either brown *Carhartt* jackets or random snowmobile winter attire. The air was redolent with cigarette smoke, stale beer and body odor. A splendid time is guaranteed for all, Maurice thought to himself as he forced a wide smile.

Toby Keith's *"Should've been a cowboy"* seemed to come to a screaming halt, along with all conversation and action inside the dimly lit bar. Maurice could almost swear you could hear his sweat splattering on the well-worn wooden floor. All those white, sweaty, red faces were all turned toward him. His stomach churned and he felt bile fight its way up his throat and wash around in the back of his mouth. He continued to force a smile. He knew he looked like a lone raisin in a basket full of flour but he tried to keep calm. The clinking of glasses and plinking of quarters into the jukebox broke the tension and Maurice could feel his body leaning toward the door. He slowly stepped back and his movement suddenly stopped.

"Gotta stay for at least one drink Mooooooorice." Butch's Jack-O-Lantern smile seemed too wide and his wide body blocked any escape Maurice had hoped to find.

"Merry Christmas everybody," Ashley belted and threw her arms wide open, mimicking a huge hug to the entire bar. He couldn't help but watch her ass in her tight jeans and *Lugz* boots. He'd never seen such a beautiful woman and the thought of being engaged to her made his member swell. He quickly moved his hands in front of his crotch. He kept smiling. Butch shuffled forward and Maurice felt himself move forward as well. Ashley grabbed him by his shaking arm and made for the bar.

The twangy refrain of Tim McGraw's *"Live like you're dying"* seemed to shake the patrons and the frivolity resumed. The rowdiness continued and laughter filled the country bar but Maurice could still feel the steely gaze upon him as they made their way through the thick crowd and to the pool-room of the bar. Many smiles, hugs, and kisses were given to his blonde bride but it seemed like he didn't exist as they moved toward the back room.

"Heya, Ash, the usual, kid?" a short, shaggy salt and pepper haired lady asked from behind the bar with a twisty smile.

"You betchyur ass Bessie . . . hook me and my man up," Ashley smiled and pushed on through the glad-handing crowd. The yellowish lights from the Genesee Cream Ale light hanging from the pool table washed out the whiteness even more from the people in the bar as Maurice excused himself as his fiancé forged her way past them. The stares continued. Maurice could almost feel the crowd closing in. He hoped it was just his paranoia creeping in.

The pool-room was packed and beyond it lay the doors to the smoker's deck outside. A tall, lanky man in a leather vest tossed his pool cue onto the table, sending the balls scattering. He adjusted his long reddish-brown ponytail and smiled as he saw Ashley making her way through the crowd. A short, pudgy patron with a waist long mullet threw up his fat arms in protest. The tall man ignored him.

"Hey heaven, you been a long time gone, sexy," he said and stepped between Ashley and Maurice.

3.

"Don't Pass Me By"

"Hey Scooter, what's new?" Ashley feigned interest. Her movement halted by the lanky biker blocking her way into the back room.

"Not a thing baby; missed ya though. You never said goodbye when ya ran off last summer. Trying to hurt my feelings, or what?" Scooter DeRueter's two missing front teeth made his esses sound serpentine.

Maurice tried to catch up to his fiancé but a tussle over the next quarter on the pool table blocked his passage. The jukebox sounded like it was turned up to eleven and Keith Urban twanged about how someone looked good in his shirt. The song, setting and crowd made his dark skin crawl. He had a bad feeling about this whole 'telling the parents' thing. Still, he was here; like it or not. He faked his best polite smile and tried to keep his eye on Ashley and avoid the glaring eyes of the all-Caucasian crowd.

"Excuse me, please," he said, but it was lost amongst the din of the country music and shouting around the pool table. He was beginning to lose his composure. Three large good ol' boys shot him a death look and stopped their fighting over the pool table. Maurice wished they didn't do that.

"I'm thinkin' you owe me at *least* a kiss, Ash." He grabbed her with his long, boney fingers and smiled. His pale, freckled skin seemed ghostly in the light from the bluish beer sign hanging on the wall next to the dartboard. He already looked half-dead; with his almost translucent skin wrapped tightly over the cheekbones. She tried to pull away.

"Now come on, hon, you could at least buy a lady a drink first." She winked and pulled away. It was too late. He held her in his skeletal grasp. He smiled.

She felt bile rise in the back of her throat.

"Well, when you left Ash, you kinda left things . . . undone." Scooter's flirtatious smile transformed into a sneer. His boney grip bore into her tender, pale skin.

Maurice noticed, tensed and clinched his fists. He found himself between a younger looking man wearing an Arcadia Falls Wrestling t-shirt and backwards New York Yankees ball cap. On the other side of the human blockade was the short portly pool player. He closed in on Maurice, cocked his head back, and smiled. The flab of his arms oozed through the worse-for-wear, yellow stained long underwear sleeves. He pushed up his coke-bottle glasses and spat a brown wad onto the worn linoleum floor. A long, brown trail of spit slowly dripped from his unshaven face.

Maurice began to sweat. It felt like someone cranked the heat up to eighty. He wasn't sure if it was the mass of bodies in the small bar or his anger brewing inside him as he watched the scarecrow-looking motherfucker molesting his woman. The anger surprised him. He usually had a low boiling point, but this piece of shit redneck was pushing his luck. The lanky bastard dropped his skeletal hand down and grabbed Ashley's ass and Maurice could feel his temples throb. He lunged forward; his efforts were stopped by the fat pool player with the Jeff Gordon 24 ball cap.

"What ya doin', bro? Can't ya see we're in the

middle of a game here?" His breath stank of onion rings and beer. The leftover spittle lashed out toward Maurice as he spoke. The words seemed to drip with contempt and condescension. Maurice was damn sure this walking dung pile didn't even know what condescension meant. He turned his head, took a deep breath, and turned back to his odious obstacle.

"All I see is a drunk, ignorant fuck that's about to get his fat ass handed to him if he doesn't get out of my way," Maurice spat, his gaze slowly breaking from Ashley and finally freezing on the Jeff Gordon fan in front of him. The fat man just smirked. The peach fuzz on his chin jiggled as he shook his head.

"Now see, that's just what I'd expect from a nig . . ."

"Nah, no worries boss, Teddy here is shit-faced, don't worry about him, man." The young kid patted Maurice on the shoulder and offered a pacifying smile. Maurice wasn't buying it or giving a shit. He focused on the scrawny scarecrow feeling up his fiancé's ass, and wondered if he truly had a brain.

4.

"Get Back"

"I'm gonna stomp a mud hole in your already brown ass boy," The fat pool player grunted and shoved Teddy aside and rushed at Maurice. It all happened so fast. Maurice grabbed him by his dirty shirt, sidestepped and shoved him towards the jukebox. His large frame slammed into the jukebox and made Taylor Swift skip a beat. That's the best she's ever sounded, Maurice laughed and turned his head on swivel. He didn't have much time to waste. He hated to fight, especially when the nasty-ass rednecks could be his fiancé's family. Hell, they're all probably related anyway. His laugh was cut short by a blur of motion from his right. He could hear Ashley screaming for them to stop. It was no use. He squatted down; a large hairy-knuckled fist nearly took his head clean off. He knew he needed to make this quick and try and get the hell out of there before all of the inbred hicks piled on top of him.

He swung his fist upward and caught his attacker with an uppercut. It caught the drunkard off guard and Maurice saw blood, mixed with white and yellow shards, exit the staggering man's gaping mouth. He knew this was his chance. He shot a risky look at Ashley; she was crying and being held with her arms across her body. Scooter the 'scarecrow' held her fast and just glared at Maurice with a yellow- and brown-toothed grin. She fought for release, but it was no use. Maurice could hear her protesting and begging them to stop. That wasn't working either. He saw a narrow gap in the crowd from whence they came in and saw the glowing red of the exit sign. This was his last chance to get the hell out of here while still walking upright. The entire bar area was hooting and hollering, calling for his ass to be kicked and giving the brawlers tips on the best way to *get 'er done*. He found his first movement was toward the gap. He then froze as all the shouting and country music seemed to stop. All sound became isolated as Ashley's begging cries were the only thing inside his head. His next move was to his left, toward the fat pool player and the Scarecrow squeezing the daylights out of his woman, his fiancée'.

"Whoa, are ya gonna pay for that, bro!" the fat man yelled, but Maurice couldn't hear him. His focus was on Ashley and the fastest way to get to her. A sharp pain filled the left side of his face and his eye began to swell shut. He staggered and caught himself on the edge of the pool table. The roar from the crowd brought him back to his senses and he could feel the big man lumbering for him. Maurice snatched up the pool cue that was lying atop the pool table and swung it in a wide arc in the fat man's direction. His hands vibrated as the stick made contact and the crowd let out a collective *ooooohhhhhhh*, as if the air was let out of a huge tractor tire. Maurice regained his balance and stepped over the knocked out pool player. He almost tripped on his large, rotund belly. But his *Timberland* hiker found purchase on the wet tiled floor. He looked around and held the broken pool cue like a sword in front of him. He could feel the heat from the jukebox against his back; his chest rose and fell quick, and he could feel his pulse pounding in his temples. The neon lights from the multitude of beer signs made his head ache and his eyes burned with pain. He tightened the grip on the shattered pool stick and turned as he heard Ashley screaming.

The crowd rose back to its frenzied pitch just as his left eye slammed completely shut from the fat man's sucker punch.

The jukebox cranked out *"Boot scootin' Boo-gie."* It startled Maurice and he jumped, almost losing grip on the stick. Two of the fat man's friends grit their summer-teeth, punched their hands, and slowly approached him. He tensed and swung that stick back like a Louisville slugger.

"Okay, knock that shit off, *goddammit,*" a loud, deep booming voice filled the bar and made Maurice cringe; he thought he knew the voice, and waited for the piling on to begin.

"Scooter, if ya don't get yur goddamn dickskinners off my daughter, I'm gonna gut you like a fuckin' pig." The booming voice belonged to an even bigger man.

Maurice tensed and turned to face the entrance to the back room. A man, far bigger than the ox that greeted them at the door, stood staring at the redneck scarecrow manhandling Ashley. He had to duck to avoid rapping his head on the doorway. He didn't look pleased.

"Daddy!" Ashley screamed and broke free from Scooter, who was trembling, and Maurice could have sworn he saw a wet stain beginning to spreading on the dirtbags ragged jeans. He smiled.

Daddy stepped into the room and somehow it seemed to shrink. The colors washed out and the lights dimmed. The bar crowd around the pool table scrambled out and funnelled into the main bar area — leaving only Ashley, Scooter, *'Jeff Gordon'* and Maurice. This wasn't the way he wanted to meet his future father-in-law. Yet, here he was.

"Daddy, I've missed you so much." Ashley ran to the big man, wearing a black *Carhartt* bib overalls and a red and blue shirt, over white long underwear. He was clean-shaven, save for solid white muttonchops. His big head was shaved clean as Mr. Clean and looked like he could clean up just about anything he set his mind to. Maurice swallowed hard, took a deep breath, and rubbed his swelling eye.

"Oh, Daddy, I've got someone you have to meet." She looked to Maurice and her large brown eyes seemed to calm his nerves and make him all warm inside. As they always did. The big man released his clinging daughter and slowly walked toward Maurice. It was then that Maurice began to worry about a piss stain appearing on his own pants. Nothing came, and for that he was grateful. He stood straight up and tried to look tough. It didn't work.

"Who the hell are you?" Daddy questioned and shoved a big hand into Scooter's chest, sending him tumbling into the popcorn machine. A small round of laughter could be heard from the main bar- room. Daddy shot them a look and all fell silent. He turned his attention back to Maurice and his grimace didn't change. Someone shouted something about kicking his ass, but Maurice tried to ignore it.

"Uh, he's Maurice, Daddy," Ashley said and ran to put herself between her imposing father and nervous fiancé. "Maurice Ware, yeah, I told you about him, Daddy. He's the guy from North Carolina and he goes to Naz with me. He's a musician." Her voice was slathered in desperation and hope. Maurice was praying that hope would win out, but he wasn't placing any bets.

"Ah, so you some kinda rapper or sum shit, Mooooorice?" Daddy said as he leaned down and looked deep into Maurice's dark brown eyes. He stood a good foot taller than him and at least two feet wider as well. He used his bulk to his oppressive advantage.

"No sir, I *hate* rap. I feel it leads to . . . deeper acceptance of . . . the ignorant theory that all black men are angry or trying to get something for nothing." Maurice tightened his jaw and stared the big man in the eye and answered.

"And my Momma brought me up thinkin' that every man must make his own path in life and that nobody owes me anything." He finished with a rising confident tone.

Daddy stood straight up and took a deep breath and it seemed like an hour passed before he spoke or a noise was let loose inside the bar. The jukebox fell silent and the entire bar-room seemed to take a collective breath.

"So, Mooooorice, are you . . . dating my Punkin?" Daddy's bright blue eyes grew wide as he waited for the answer.

"Well sir, I . . . uh . . . Yes . . . me . . . um . . . "

The crowd that was held at bay began to swarm in, their angry faces and muddled comments began to become a roar, and they surrounded Maurice.

He didn't like where this was headed. He felt his ass tighten and knew that a slight piss stain was about to be the least of his concerns.

Daddy leaned close, his sharply-bent wide nose, that Maurice could tell had been broken many times, touched his. The big man's breath stunk of beer and cigar smoke. Daddy's harsh eyes squinted and his thick white, bushy eyebrows furrowed as he gritted his teeth and shoved a large, stubby finger into Maurice's quivering chest. The only sounds in the bar-room were that of a few hushed *"get 'em"* and *'kick his ass'*.

A glass mug shattered the silence as the bar-tender dropped it on the hard wooden floor.

Daddy grabbed Maurice with his left hand and he noticed it was missing its index finger and only a stub was on the middle one. Daddy's grip was still strong and jolts of pain shot through Maurice's shoulder, up into his neck. Daddy pressed in even closer.

Maurice's jaw clenched and he slowly raised the broken pool cue; he readied it to fend off the big man. He saw something from the corner of his eye and it slowed his heart even more. Ashley's beautiful, pale face broke into a wide smile. He felt his stomach gurgle and bile raced for the back of his throat. *What the fuck is going on?* he thought as panic filled his mind.

5.

"Fool on the Hill"

"I hear you want to marry my Ashley-girl, is that true, Mooooorice?" Daddy inquired, never moving, and maintaining his intense stare.

"Yesss . . . S . . . ir . . . I . . . do . . . " Maurice managed to eke out the words.

"You better remember those words, son," Daddy bellowed and his violent sneer turned into a wide smile that matched his daughter's. He gave Maurice a quick wink and he let his tight grip on his shoulder go and pulled him into an engulfing bear hug.

"Welcome to the family, Maurice," Daddy said, and squeezed harder.

"Uh . . . oh, um . . . *thank* you, sir," Maurice was stunned and felt himself shaking and his heart decided to beat in a syncopated rhythm that would make Buddy Rich proud. His hands shook and he let the pool cue drop to the floor. Ashley ran over to him, joined in the group hug, and kissed him on the cheek. He recoiled as sharp pains blasted his swollen left eye.

"Oh, babe, I'm so sorry about that," she cooed. Kissed him again, laughing.

Daddy released him, he felt blood rush back into his right arm and the urge to piss and shit himself dissipated, and he was grateful. He still had no clue what the hell was going on. The thought must have translated into a look on his sweaty face as Daddy let out a bellowing laugh that shook the thick, smoke-treated exposed beams of the Torchlight Inn.

"Oh, we were just bustin' yer balls son." Daddy let loose another volley of belly laughs and the entire bar erupted in matching catcalls and hollers. Maurice just stood there stupefied, with a swollen shut, purple and black left eye and a bloody-knuckled right hand.

"Babe, I called Daddy and told him the day after you asked me to marry you. It was his idea to mess with you." She gently pulled on his slack jaw and forced him to look into her enthralling brown eyes. "It's his way of welcoming you into the family, babe. You thought they were all a bunch of inbred, sister boffin' rednecks, huh?" She winked and kissed his nose and hugged him close.

"They . . . *we,* are good people babe." She pulled back, looked up at her Daddy, and smiled.

"He's the one Daddy,"

"I see that, Punkin," Daddy said and pulled her close and kissed the top of her head.

"I hate to . . . um, ask but, if this was all a joke, why did those guys jump me like that?" Maurice asked, lightly touching his sensitive eye.

"Oh . . . those boys just got carried away. I reckon they been drinkin' too much Genny; nothin' new there. Sorry about that son." Daddy's bright blue eyes twinkled as he winked and slapped Maurice on the shoulder and almost knocked him to his already weak knees.

"Yeah, him and the other GU . . . "

"Nice punch. Timmy could never take a punch." Daddy laughed again, yanked Maurice away from Ashley, and pulled him toward the bar. "Woody, help those poor bastards up? They look like two goddamn turtles on their backs." Daddy's bear-like laugh filled the bar.

"Ya know, Maurice, I know we all look like

somethin' that stepped out of *Deliverance* or a Larry the Cable Guy punch line, but we are just hard workin' folks just like your family probably is, I reckon." He shot him another wink and for the first time, Maurice's heart and stomach slowed down and stopped flip-flopping. He let a smile slip out, nodded his head, and felt his feet barely touch the floor as his future father-in-law 'carried' him to the bar.

Daddy propped Maurice against the bar, offered the old bartender a soft smile, and ordered a round of drinks. Ashley followed quickly and hugged Maurice from behind.

"And hey, Bessie, can you get my future son-in-law here some ice for his shiner?" Daddy gave the short, older bartender a flirtatious wink.

"Here ya are, hon. It's gonna be a doozy too." Bessie nodded her head and handed Maurice a black checkered bar-towel full of ice. She gave him a pat on the arm, shot Big Daddy a return wink, and smiled. Her chubby cheeks turned a rosy red and she walked away down to the other side of the bar. Daddy looked at Ashley as she hopped up on a barstool next to Maurice and smiled.

"You're not mad are you?" she said. She playfully

darted her tongue in and over his ear. He shrugged and took the drink the smiling bartender placed on the bar and smiled.

"Well, meeting your fiancé's parents is a pretty scary event by normal standards. I didn't expect to get punched in the face," he answered honestly, and was surprised to hear himself chuckle. Daddy snatched his shot glass full of brown liquid with his huge hand and gave Maurice another wink.

"Son, sorry about that again, but it seems you came out on top of that exchange and I gotta say, I'm impressed. They must have taught ya well down in Durham." He smiled wide and put the shot glass to his mouth and jerked his large head back and the liquid was gone. He slammed it down on the bar and he motioned Bessie for another. He looked at Maurice and then to his full shot glass and raised a fuzzy gray eyebrow.

"That shot sure as hell ain't gonna drink itself son," he grinned, and raised the new shot glass to his lips.

Maurice nodded and swallowed the shot and slammed the glass down, only to be met by another full shot glass. Ashley let out a laugh and quickly stole the shot from his hand and swallowed it in one quick motion and let out a deep exhale as she slammed it down on the bar, next to her father's empty glass.

I can see where she gets that from, Maurice raised his eyebrow and she grabbed him in a strong hug and kissed him deeply. He could taste the whiskey as it burned his gums and tongue as she explored his mouth. She let out a low moan and they both began to smile.

"Cut that shit out you two lovebirds; this IS a public place for Christ's sake," Daddy ordered and half-smiled. "Hey Bessie, dear, could you have Ellen bring us back a couple pitchers of Genny hon?" He blew her a kiss and tossed a hundred dollar bill on the bar. "And keep 'em comin', sweetie."

"You got it, honeypie," Bessie answered and motioned to a short, young brunette at the other end of the bar.

They passed the pool table, where Scooter and another guy in snowmobile overalls were helping up the fat pool player, who was shaking his head and wiping blood from his eyes. The other guy, the one he'd knocked the fuck out, was still lying on the pool table. His scrawny, scraggly-haired girlfriend was trying to wake him up by dumping a beer over his face. It didn't work and she shot Ashley a death glare. He turned to Ashley and she just rolled her shoulders and flipped the girl off as they passed.

"Come on kids, the party's out back." Daddy grabbed Maurice by his blue winter jacket and pulled him toward the back room. "Time to meet the rest of the Vanslycke clan. You're gonna need that beer they're bringing out." He threw his head back and another belly laugh escaped from his large frame.

"He's not kidding babe," Ashley nodded and shrugged her shoulders as she followed them to the back room.

Ah swell, Maurice thought. He wished for another shot.

6.

"With a little help from my friends"

Maurice was escorted into the *'backroom'* sandwiched between Daddy on his left and Ashley on his right. They both had their arms around him. Making sure he wouldn't make a break for it. He chortled to himself. Once he got a good look inside the dimly lit room, he guessed his was right. The *'backroom'* was an outdoor deck, converted into what could best be explained as a large, three season porch. Sheets of graying plywood made crude walls halfway to the ceiling. The rest of the walls were two-by-fours and blue and black poly tarps held to the wood by screws and twist ties. Benches lined the walls and four large wooden spools acted as tables. In the center was a 50-gallon drum cut in half with a glowing red-hot fire inside of it. There were people of various sizes and sexes huddled around the heat source. Maurice quickly glanced around the room and estimated that there were at least fifty people packed into this plastic haven.

He really wanted that shot now.

"Well looky here who I found at the bar," Daddy's voice was proud and that made Maurice relax a little. Not a lot. It was enough.

The large crowd let out loud cheers, and shouts of *welcome home* Ashley rang out. The faces in the crowd were hard to make out for Maurice. The flickering yellow and red flames cast jerky shadows upon the tarps that ebbed and flowed with the powerful winter winds outside. He wasn't sure if the joke was over quite yet.

"Clear a path you dumbasses," Daddy shouted and just like a plaid, *Carhartt*-wearing Moses, the mumbling crowd split in front of them and there, hanging on the makeshift blue and black wall, was a white bed sheet. On it in orange spray paint were huge splashy letters. Ashley hugged him tight as he tried to make out just what it read. *Congratulations Ashley and Moreese!* The thin linen fought against its zip-ties, matching the movement of the tarp billowing behind it. He could feel Ashley tremble and he heard her start crying. His eyes began to water up too; he felt warm all over, and this time, he was glad it wasn't his fight-or-flight response causing his temperature changes. He was happy and seeing Ashley so happy made his swollen eye feel like such a small price to pay.

"I could really use that drink now," he joked and the smiling crowd roared with laughter. A myriad of names and greetings were thrown at him and he sure hoped he could remember them, but a combination of the punch upside his head and the shots, he feared it was just wishful thinking.

As if on perfect timing, Ellen shoved her way into the craziness of *chateau* Vanslycke, carrying two, overflowing pitchers of beer. The deafening cry filled the smoky air once more, inside the tent city of the back room.

"Oh, God bless your ever-lovin' soul, Ellen," Daddy smiled and poured four red plastic cups full of beer and handed one to Maurice and Ashley, keeping the pitcher for himself. He raised the frothy over-sized mug on high, loosed a big grin, and swooped around, trying to get each of the partygoers' attention.

Ellen shot Maurice a flirtatious smile and a wink

as she looked him up and down. He turned away, trying to ignore her.

"I have something to say, so all you assholes, shut the hell up." He chuckled and winked at Maurice and Ashley. Maurice was beginning to feel no pain and that was good. His left eye was numb from the ice and from all the tense bullshit from the confrontation, he ached all over. All the time spent in college had softened him and he feared he'd lost all his street skills from surviving in the dangerous streets of Durham. He hoped that all the "friendly jokes" were over for the night. He looked at Daddy climbed on top of a rickety-looking wooden chair and raised the pitcher of beer again. The crowd silenced and all attention turned to the big man.

"Well, it's about time ya'll shut the hell up," Daddy laughed. His barrel chest bounced and Maurice thought that the bowing chair was going to splinter into pieces and send the large man sprawling on the worn floor. However, it held; just creaked and flexed in protest. Maurice smiled and Ashley tugged on his arm and brought his attention back to Daddy in the center of the room.

"First, I want to welcome my lil' Punkin home

and it's been a long time since she headed off to school in August." Daddy looked down at Ashley and his broad jaw quivered, and Maurice could tell the big man was fighting to keep his wide smile from turning into a frown. "It was a long time to leave your old man alone." The flickering light from the fire barrel formed sharp shadows on the man's weather worn face and his deep-set blue eyes began to get misty. He took a big swig from the pitcher and a low murmur came over the crowd.

It was then that Maurice realized that Ashley never talked about her mother and when Daddy spoke of being alone, he wondered where her mother was. One thing he knew for sure was that, now wasn't the time to ask. He could feel Ashley begin to squeeze his arm tighter and she too began to cry.

"Now, this ain't no time for bein' all maudlin and all that bullshit. *Hell* no. This is time for celebration. As you all know, my baby girl is getting' married." His voice cracked. The crowd went crazy, shouting and throwing their hands up in the air. Beer, whiskey, and lord knows what other liquid flew up into the air as well and Maurice could feel the worn wooden planks on the floor shake from the cheering family.

"It's been a tough few years since Julia's been gone and I don't think I could have made it, if it weren't for Ashley-girl, here. It's been just her 'n me and I think we did okay, don't you, Punkin?" Daddy looked at Ashley and big tear-drops glistened as they fell down his smiling cheeks. Maurice was moved to see that the big man didn't give a shit about crying in front of all these people. They were family, sure, but for a rugged, tough-as-nails man as Daddy seemed to be, it was a pleasant surprise and he thought that maybe he had prejudged these 'rednecks' too soon.

All eyes were on Maurice and he subconsciously drained the remainder of his beer and wiped the foam on his jacket sleeve. Someone behind him, in a Buffalo Bills jacket, reached over and refilled his cup from his pitcher. An old man with coke-bottle lens glasses and a Santa Claus beard gave him a jack-o-lantern smile and patted him on the back.

"Uh, thanks," Maurice said. He wouldn't have normally drunk from strangers' pitcher, but hell, this night was far from normal and he didn't see it getting normal any time soon. So he toasted his new friend and took a deep drink from it.

Daddy jumped down and the entire room shuttered with the impact. The raucous crowd responded with roars and yee-haws. Maurice chuckled, but still worried that this *"jimmy-rigged"* room was going to crash to the ground.

Daddy held up his hands again and silenced the rowdy ensemble.

"Now everyone, let me introduce y'all to our newest family member." Daddy yanked Maurice from Ashley's tight embrace and pulled him to his side. He thought he felt his ribs crack and his shoulder pop from the strong man's hug. He smiled and nodded as he looked around at the full room. "This here is Maurice Ware and he has one helluva uppercut," Daddy said. His wide face grew wider into a smile and he motioned around the tarped room, waved his big hand in a swooping motion, and brought it back to Maurice's chest. That now began to rise and fall with anxiety. "And he is my soon-to-be son-in-law and a welcome addition to our insanely fucked up family." Daddy's raucous laughter was matched once again by the jovial whooping and hollering of the rest of the Vanslycke family. They all gathered in closer and raised their drink of choice. It looked like a scene straight out of a Garth Brooks' song. Cowboy hats, NASCAR jackets and Ski-doo winter jackets abound. To Maurice's surprise and stunned impression, they were all welcoming and embracing him. His color didn't seem to matter, his breath caught in his chest and he, too, began to cry.

7.

"I'm a Loser"

Cody Reynolds really needed a smoke. The damn laws in New York, just like every other goddamned place in the country, prohibited him from the joys of his precious nicotine. He didn't really want to venture out in the cold. He'd spent the better part of the night working on Patti Pierce and it had been a long drought for him. He really needed to get *laid*. The bar was packed and there was some kinda bullshit party going on in the backroom and that's where the smokers usually went to get their fix on. Not tonight though. He knew that if he left Patti for two seconds, one of the other douche-bags would flock to her hot ass, like a deer to a damn salt lick. He would be damned if he was gonna let that happen. His dry period was ending tonight, even if it killed him. He leaned in and kissed Patti on her fake tanned cheek and she smiled and licked his pug nose and gave it a fake bite. He smiled.

"Hey darlin', I need to go grab a quick smoke, why don't ya grab us another round and play some tunes on the jukebox." He winked and threw a twenty on the bar and pulled her close and cradled her wide ass in her tight fitting Levi's. She let go a soft moan, shoved her wide tongue into his small mouth, grabbed his crotch, and giggled.

"Sure thing, hon. Hurry back though. You don't want me gettin' cold and lonely now, do ya?" She patted his ass as he kicked the bar stool back and headed for the door. He knew he shouldn't leave and he felt his crotch throb and he was determined to get some tonight. The biting Canadian gale pushed him back as he opened the door. The snow felt like a million minuscule needles piercing his exposed skin. He pulled his Mack Tools hoodie over his head, zipped up his leather jacket, and stepped out into the frigid night. Another powerful gust yanked the door from his hands and it slammed shut. He came to the abrupt decision he needed to quit smoking or it would be the death of him. He adjusted the bulge in his pants and squinted through the pelting snow to see where he'd parked his truck. He ran toward the back of the parking lot, by the snow-buried volleyball court.

He hurried past a late seventies Chevy van covered in at least three inches of snow. He thought he saw movement, but he was too damn cold and needed a smoke too bad to give a shit. He squeezed his way past a Dodge Neon that was parked extremely close to his truck and opened the door. It creaked open in protest, and he climbed inside and slammed it shut.

His cold hands shook as he dug deep into his jacket for the keys. They found purchase on the Stewie Griffin key-chain and he plucked the keys out and shoved it into the ignition. The old engine shuddered, hesitated and roared to life. Cody prayed for heat. It was slow to come, but he was cheered up that he remembered he had a bottle of Captain Morgan tucked behind the seat. He felt with his numb fingers and let out a big laugh as he found the cold bottle. He brought it out, twisted the cap off, and took a sip. Satisfied, he fetched a Doral menthol from his jacket pocket and pushed the lighter in on the truck's ashtray. To hold him over, he took another swig and turned the radio on. Tom T. Hall crooned about how he liked beer, and it made Cody chuckle. He hiccupped and took another drink from the bottle. He almost pissed himself as a rapping on his driver-side window echoed through the small cab. He almost dropped the whiskey bottle and he pulled a juggling act just to make sure he didn't dump it out on the passenger seat. It's a good thing he caught it too, because the last thing he needed was to be pulled over and nailed for another DWI. This one would send his happy ass to jail for a long while. He felt a trickle of piss spread across his worn jeans. He fumbled with the bottle and capped it, then shoved it under the seat, bitching and grumbling all the while. He grabbed a few leftover McDonald's napkins and dabbed at his wet crotch. He really hoped it wasn't the cops and would have given anything for a piece of fucking gum or a breath mint.

The rapping came again, heavier, more insistent this time. He flicked the radio off and cranked the window down half way, so as not to let all the warm air out. Cody could barely see anything through the near-white-out conditions.

"Yeah, yeah, gimme a damn second, Jesus fuckin' Christ," Cody shouted over the howling winds. He shoved the cigarette into his mouth and stared at the lighter in the ashtray impatiently. He gave his best fake smile and turned to the window as snow filled the opening. He wasn't quite sure if what he was seeing was real, or a trick of the snowstorm or the result of too much booze, but he could swear that the face in his window was that of *Paul McCartney*. He shook his head and looked again. He stared out the window, his mouth dropped open, and the cigarette hung from his bottom lip, dangled down, and bounced against his chin. The figure standing outside his window *was* Paul fucking McCartney.

The strong winds pounded at Cody's small truck and the flip-flapping trench coat of the *Beatle* standing outside it cast jagged shadows from the dusk-to-dawn lights high above and behind it. The figure blotted out the light and its features were hiding in the blackness of its shadow. Cody chuckled and, seeing as it wasn't a cop, reached back behind the seat and pulled out the bottle of rum. The figure laughed and it floated off into the wintry mix of snow and ice consuming the entire area. The laughter seemed to be followed by a familiar song. *Damn familiar,* Cody thought as he smiled at the stranger and took a sip from the bottle.

Cody rolled the window down the rest of the way; a biting gust of wind knocked his ball cap off, and it smacked against the passenger side window. He heard a feminine giggle come from the shadowy stranger. The lilting strains of oboes and harpsichords came through the window on the crisp wind. *I know that song,* he thought again.

"What's shakin'?" Cody asked. He nodded and took another sip from the bottle of rum.

"Good evening, Sir, might I bother you for a fag?" A soft, but curt voice asked and leaned into the window, exposing its face.

"You *are* fuckin' *Paul McCartney*," Cody exclaimed with a raspy laugh and kept nodding his head in justification.

"Well, not quite love, but for tonight, it will do," the feminine voice grew louder to compete with the raging storm. The pale white of the *Paul* mask seemed to glow inside the cab. The figure reached in with a slender, leather-sleeved arm and caressed Cody's face and let loose a giggle. Cody felt his member stiffen inside his jeans.

"I was hoping you would share some of that

bottle with me, love," she said and traced her leather-gloved hand from his cheek, down his arm, onto his stomach and then his bulging pants. *Paul* looked at Cody, laughed again, and traced her finger back up the half-empty bottle.

"Uh, yeah, sure, plenty here to go around sweetie." Cody's voice shook and the figure snatched the bottle from his quivering hand. The all-too familiar tune finally came to his memory and he smiled as a gloved hand caressed his hard package.

"*...Helter Skelter!*" Cody's mind raced and smiled with final recognition.

He suddenly became colder and Cody couldn't feel his hand as it flopped down onto the leather seat. The familiar song grew louder as the inside of the windshield gushed with a red substance, like someone had taken a paint bucket and tossed its contents all over it. A warm sensation came back to his body, along with a ringing laughter. The color of the windshield was red . . . *blood* red. Cody's breath caught in his throat and his heartbeat waned. It was *his* blood.

"What's wrong, love? Feeling a little . . . low?" *Paul's* voice grew as cold and numb as the harsh winter air filling the cab. Blood rained from the large gash in Cody's throat. The leather-clad hand held a long, crimson-colored blade and it bobbed up and down to the final chorus of The Beatles' "*Helter Skelter.*"

Cody felt numb all over; his limp head dropped against his chest, and he watched as *Paul McCartney* opened up the door, unzipped his blood-soaked jeans, and yanked out his limp penis. The chalky-white mask looked up at his blinking, fading eyes, sliced the loose skin of his scrotum and penis, and yanked it from his limp body. His senses were fading, but he heard the opening lines of "*Hello, goodbye*" as the bloody and mangled pieces of his manhood were dangled in front of him. Then all things went dark.

He heard laughter. *Sir Paul* wasn't alone . . .

8.

"I don't want to spoil the party"

The doors slammed shut and the deeply piled snow glistened as it flitted into the florescent lights of the dusk-to-dawn Torchlight Inn's parking lot. Only two sounds filled the cold night; the thumping bass line of *"John* Deere Green" filtering out of the bar and the chambering of shotguns. Somewhere off in the wintry distance, a lone dog barked. It sounded hollow and melancholy.

The man in the lead pulled his mask down over his large face and stopped before the almost snowed-in entrance to the bar. The odd shape created an even odder shadow on the step before him.

"Check your gear, mates." His tone as cold as the whipping Lake Ontario wind as it lapped at the four figures all dressed in black fur and ankle-length, leather jackets...

The quartet examined their weapons. Shotguns, extra shells, nylon rope and machetes were all in their proper place. Then they pulled down their masks and a loud, collective laughter joined the crying canine and was lost in the raging snowstorm racing in from the lake.

The hard packed snow crunched underneath their sleek black boots as they approached the pulsating bar. Large, dime-sized snowflakes fell from the black sky and cut visibility close to zero, creating a white curtain in front them. The red and blue neon beer signs acted like beacons and targets in the brisk night.

The four figures stood to attention in front of the green van and the lead figure examined them from head to toe. He adjusted his *John Lennon* mask and gave an approving nodded.

He looked them over. A very large man, nearly reaching the top of the van, stood with his broad chest pushed outward. *John* surveyed the big man and patted him on the chest. The man-mountain nodded; his *Ringo Starr* mask and his barrel chest seemed to protrude even more into the night's frigid air.

John continued down the line to a small, but lithe frame. He took his time observing the curvaceous figure donning a *Paul McCartney* mask. She was well equipped and covered in fresh blood. She held a glob of flesh in her right, gloved hand.

He was happy and moved on.

A very athletic figure finished *John's* examination. *George Harrison* stood tall, erect, and ready for action. He was happy.

John turned and walked to the door of the Torchlight Inn. He faced his compatriots. His long black fur jacket flowed in the harsh wind, exposing the multi-colored pants beneath. He pumped the shotgun, reached into the jacket, and fetched out a white object. He turned the iPod on and the beginning traffic noises of *Sgt. Pepper's Lonely Hearts Club Band* filled his wireless ear buds. The three followed suit and placed their earpieces in.

"You all look fabulous. Let's knock them dead, mates." His voice was as cold as the northeast gusts assailing the bar. Finished, he nodded, turned, grabbed the metal handle of the door, and yanked it open.

No one heard the little bells jingle-jangle as the *Frightful Four* entered the packed, loud bar.

9.

"Come Together"

"Babe, I told you they were awesome," Ashley gushed and downed another shot. She was shit-faced and he knew it. However, this was a night of celebration and far be it from him to put an end to it. He was just so happy it didn't end up with him getting his ass kicked, or worse. It troubled him thinking that way, and he had fought those thoughts and feelings from day one of their relationship. Nevertheless, they were there, whether he liked them or not. He figured he would have to wrestle with those emotions and suck them up. He loved Ashley and would do anything to make her happy. Daddy shoved another shot in front of him and winked. Maurice of course, obliged.

"They are great, kiddo," he said and gave her a

kiss on the cheek. She yanked him in close, digging her bright pink fingernails into the back of his neck. Her perky nipples poked through the Nazareth College long-sleeve t-shirt. She cooed and kissed him hard. A rowdy call filled the makeshift backroom, followed by laughter and dirty catcalls. Daddy laughed loudly and patted Maurice on the shoulder, interrupting their little moment.

"Heads up, son, you got eyes on ya." Daddy leaned in and pointed back toward the pool table area. Scooter stood, leaning against the pool table, his arms crossed. He was drinking a Budweiser. His deep-set eyes were fixed on the entwined lovers. The fat pool dude leaned into his ear and whispered something while dabbing a red-stained bar towel on his head. Maurice knew the night was far from over. He didn't give a rat's ass. He wouldn't let a couple of drunken idiots ruin his fiancé's night.

"Let's get another round, Ash," he turned to her and smiled. Even three sheets to the wind, she was still the most beautiful woman he'd ever seen. Her long blonde hair tussled to one side as she shot him a wide smile and bit her lower lip. She knew that drove him crazy. She *always* drove him crazy. He laughed and, for the first time that night, didn't feel self-conscious. Screw Scooter and his lard-ass pal, he thought and motioned toward the bar. He grabbed her by the hand and made their way to the poolroom. Van Morrison's "Tupelo Honey" began playing on the jukebox and Maurice nodded with approval. Ashley was as sweet as Tupelo Honey and he felt deep warmth grow inside his stomach and spread all over. He was happy, and buzzed. He laughed. Ashley joined him, in perfect timing, as they squeezed past Scooter and the portly pal. Scooter's deep-set eyes never left Maurice. That made him chuckle as he continued toward the bar.

"Howdy, fellas," Maurice nodded at Scooter and the pool guy, and smiled. Ashley shot him a wink and grinned. Scooter's face flushed red and his bright blue eyes bulged with anger. The bloody pool guy continued whispering in his ear. The minute the words came out of his mouth, Maurice knew it was stupid. He should be trying to keep things smooth, not be a smart ass. He knew better. He spotted an opening at the bar, handed Ashley a twenty-dollar bill, and pointed at the lucky opening.

"Hey Ash, that was a douchebag move, why don't you grab a couple beers for your friends there. I'm going to talk to them."

"Are you sure you want to do that babe?" Ashley cocked her head to one side, her blonde locks falling playfully across her right eye. Again with the biting of the lip, he thought.

"Yeah, I should at least give it a try." He slapped her on the ass and she hopped, then ran for the open slot with her arm raised high, flashing the money to Bessie for service.

Maurice turned on his heel and walked back to Scooter and Pool-Guy. He stuck his hand out to Scooter, whose eyes still had a bead on him.

"Hey guys, just wanted to say sorry about all . . . *that.*" He motioned to Pool-Guy's bloody scalp and offered them a slight smile. His hand was still held out in front of Scooter, waiting for reciprocation.

"Hear that, Sacks. Moooooorice here is sorry." Scooter's gaze stayed fixed on Maurice. He spit a gob of brown goo onto the floor, nearly hitting his shoe; and smiled back at him. He finished his beer and set it down on the green felt of the pool table, interrupting a game between two local under-aged high school kids. They just raised their shoulders in a "what the hell?" gesture and tossed their cues on the table, grabbed their beers and walked out into the back room.

"Now, I'm not trying to be a jerk, guys. I get it was all a joke and we all got carried away." Maurice moved his hand and made a wide-open gesture. "I know y'all been friends with Ashley forever and I just want to be cool with the people that mean a lot to her, know what I'm saying?" he said and tried to hide his indignation at the rebuffing of his handshake offer.

Scooter stood up, put his thin hands on his hips, and smiled wide. He loomed a good half foot taller than Maurice and took a step closer.

"*Friends*, huh? Is that what she told you we were?" He leaned down, tilted his thin head to the side, and had a crooked smirk on his face. Maurice could smell the cheap beer and ass stench of chewing tobacco on his breath. "Me and Ash, yeah, we were much more than *that*, Moooooorice," he snapped and sent an umber-colored wad onto the floor next to Maurice's foot.

"Ya don't say?" Maurice took a deep breath and tried hard not to show that Scooter had gotten his *goat,* as his Mother always said. He held his breath, trying not to inhale the foul stench of Scooter's mouth. "Well, that was then and this is now,

Scooter, and I'm here just to offer a handshake and a drink."

"Here we go boys, drink up." Ashley couldn't have had better timing, Maurice thought; a smile broke through his anger and he helped her with the drinks she was carrying. He grabbed two cold bottles of Bud, offered them to Scooter and the Pool-Guy. He stared straight in their eyes, and grinned.

"As I was saying, a peace-offering guys." He held out the dripping beer bottles and offered his best, *come on* grin. Ashley leaned into him, flashed her long eyelashes, and threw out her best pouting lips.

The sound of the harmonic slide guitar of the Allman Brothers' "*Old Friend*" broke the tension. Scooter's hard exterior broke, and he dropped his shoulders, grinned and gave a wink to Ashley. He reached out, snagged the beer from Maurice, and patted him on the shoulder.

"Just fuckin' with ya, bro. No hard feelings," Scooter slurred and looked at his pouting, pudgy friend. "Well, 'cept maybe *his* sorry ass." He laughed and gripped tightly onto Maurice's shoulder leaning into him.

The battered Pool-Guy reluctantly took the beer

from Maurice and quickly stepped back against the comfort of the pool table. Maurice and Scooter chuckled, and he took the drink Ashley offered him.

"Ah come on, Sacks, Whaddya want the guy to do? You charged him like a goddamn bull-moose, for fuck's sake." Scooter held onto Maurice and reached out with his left arm and snatched Sacks by the scruff of his neck and pulled him closer, laughing all the while.

"Heya fellas, drink up. This *is* a party after all . . . MY PARTY!" Ashley whooped, hollered, and fell into the three interlocked drinkers. They all collapsed into each other in a buzzed, laughing, weaving unit.

"That it is darlin', and here's to you and your man, Maurice here," Scooter let Maurice and Sacks loose and helped her gain her balance. He picked up his beer from the pool table and raised it high and lifted his sharp-angled chin with it.

"I hope you guys are happy. And Maurice, you better take damn good care of my gal here. She's the best thing that every came outta this shithole town." His words caught in his throat and Maurice could tell he was fighting tears back.

"Oh, I will, Scooter, trust me. I'm not letting her go." He clunked his bottle against Scooter's and Sacks reluctantly joined in. Ashley began shaking her hips to Kid Rock's "*All Summer Long*". She looked at her *boys* and smiled, stood on her tiptoes and clanked her bottle with theirs.

"Well if I'm not the luckiest girl in the whole world." She kept seductively swaying her hips to the thumping sounds of sampled Lynyrd Skynyrd and Warren Zevon. She bumped her hips into Maurice and it sent him bashing into Scooter as they were both drinking their beers. A spray of golden liquid splashed over them. They laughed even harder, and they staggered and fought to catch their balance.

Scooter pulled Maurice into him and his fuzzy eyes fought to find purchase on him.

"I gotta tell ya something'." He looked around, looked at Ashley then back to Maurice. "The kick in the nuts is, Mo; I bet you were thinkin' Ash and I were an item or somethin', huh?" He tilted the beer bottle back and smirked, then swallowed.

"Uh, well, yeah, I did," Maurice answered and raised an eyebrow. He looked at Ashley who lost in a world of booze and grinding to the music.

He didn't know whether to bust Scooter in the mouth in a jealous rage or throw her down right then and there on the pool table. He laughed to himself, as he had always known he was a lover not a fighter. He turned his attention back to Scooter, who was enjoying the tension-filled, pregnant pause.

"Go on . . . " Maurice accentuated his impatience with a smile and a big swig from his beer, draining it.

"Haaaaaaaaa, I like you Maurice, you're alright, bro," Scooter slapped Maurice on the back and the force made him stagger forward into Ashley, who was eyeing the table next to them. He grabbed onto her and they both let out a wild, drunken laugh.

"Nah, nah, come here, I gotta tell ya." Scooter pulled Maurice away from Ashley and they slammed into each other.

"Okay, okay. What the hell *is* it? Were you guys engaged or something?" Maurice really wanted another beer and wanted his new redneck friend to get to the damn point even more.

"No bro . . . that's the fuckin' joke!" Scooter covered his smiling face, leaned into Maurice, and let out a hissing laugh.

"As fuckin' ironic as it sounds bro, she's my sister." He leaned back and howled until his hat fell off his balding head.

Maurice just stood there dumbfounded, his mouth hanging open. Sacks belted out a laugh as well, not even having a damn clue as to why.

"We just really wanted to mess with you, bro." Scooter kept laughing and pulled at his long pony tail and motioned with his eyes toward his ball cap on the floor. Sacks swallowed his beer, bent down, and grunted as he picked it up and handed it to Scooter.

"It's okay, y'all had me for sure, Scooter, and I think we need another round, don't you?" Maurice was trying to be a good sport but he was in need of another social lubricant. He didn't give Scooter a chance to respond and headed for the bar. He caught Ashley standing on top of the table next to the ladies' room, grinding and swaying to some generic country song. They all sounded the same to him. She was having fun and he needed a drink . . . fast. He slithered his way through the packed bar and his hands found purchase on the faux-leather railing. The entire place was in a frenzy. He never thought that when he saw the poorly-lit sign that read, "The Torchlight Inn", it would be such a packed and crazy crowd. As he waited for one of the two overworked bartenders to get to him, he looked about the small but hectic bar and continued to be amazed and bewildered at the way the evening had transpired. Despite being slugged in the jaw, which was no big deal where he came from, he couldn't have hoped it would have turned out better. Despite the fact that as he looked around it looked like a Ku Klux Klan meeting in blue jeans and winter jackets. These people seemed to be just like the folks back home in North Carolina. They were just honest, hardworking people. Even as buzzed as he was; he felt ashamed that he had judged them without giving them a chance. He really needed a drink. He waved the twenty-dollar bill out, trying hard to get Bessie's attention. Ellen appeared out of the cooler, looking angry and frustrated.

"Ellen," Maurice shouted, impressed that he even remembered her name. He leaned over the bar, trying to get her attention.

She caught him and looked pissed off, but seeing it was Maurice she transformed her grimace into a smile. She came to him and leaned in, turned her ear toward him to hear over the twangy Rascal Flats song blasting through the bar.

"Uh, what do you need, honey?" she said. He could hear the aggravation in her voice and noticed Bessie was knee-deep with the flailing wall of arms, hands and dollar bills.

"What's wrong," he leaned in and yelled.

"Ah, the damn Golden Anniversary keg is kicked and I can't lift the new one, and all these assholes want more beer." She forced a smile and motioned toward the cooler behind her.

He looked at the throng of thirsty patrons and the overwhelmed old lady trying to placate them. He turned back to Ashley; she was busting a move to the crappy music, and Scooter caught him looking, held two fingers up, and smiled. She was safe, he thought, and turned back to Ellen as she placed a cold Bud in front of him. He smiled and leaned in again toward her.

"You want me to give you a hand with the keg?" he shouted, and took a quick sip of the beer. It tasted good and the coolness felt soothing against his throat.

He could see the relief flush over her pale, freckled face and she smiled, nodded in acceptance.

She brought her hands up in a thank you prayer gesture.

"Oh, thanks so much, that would be so great," she yelled over the twangy music and smiled.

He hopped over the bar, grabbed his beer and followed Ellen into the cooler. The large silver door slowly closed behind them.

10.

"Hello, Goodbye"

*P*aul held fast onto the limp, blood-dripping penis as the door to the bar shut behind her. She could still feel the heat from the facile member in her gloved hand. She salivated and eyed the throbbing crowd inside the Torchlight Inn. She smiled up at *John*, as she felt a warm wetness grow in her groin. *John* sniffed the air, peered down, and shook his masked head. She giggled and shoved the flaccid, bloody member into her breast pocket; small, wriggly red veins and nerves jutted out, hung loosely over the black pocket, and bounced as she stepped into the bar. A few of the drunken patrons in front of the door laughed and pointed and slapped one another on the backs at the odd sight as the four lads from Liverpool made their entrance.

John put his hands on his black clad hips,

surveyed their new surroundings, and sucked in a deep breath. The other three fanned out behind him. The staggering, laughing crowd parted and welcomed them in with smiles and raised glasses. *John* raised his right arm and pointed at the door. *Ringo* nodded and locked it. *George* gave him a hand, and with a huge grunt hefted the large wooden shuffleboard table and jammed it in front of the exit. *John*'s gaze went from one end of the bar to the other. Checking for other points of entry or exit. He snapped his fingers and *Paul* shot a look, followed her boss's pointed finger, and went straight to the jukebox.

The four walked onto the small dancefloor, it was well worn and the wooden underlay could be seen through some of the cracked and missing tiles. The rest of the ageing tiles were pock-marked with holes and black boot smudges. The dark, wood-planked walls of the bar made it seem to shrink as the last refrains of Big and Rich's "*Save a horse, ride a cowboy*" came to a digital halt. The rowdy crowd groaned and collectively bitched at the sudden stoppage of shit-kicking, party music and the entire attention of the bar turned toward the cleared dance floor.

John snatched up a small table and hopped up on it. His black, thick-heeled, pointed boots slid slightly as he landed. He pin-wheeled his arms as he gained his balance. His Lennon mask held frozen in a stoic grin. The restless crowd let out a loud laugh as he held his arms out wide in a 'ta-da' gesture. It was met with another round of cheering and laughs. No one seemed to notice the barricaded door or even cared about the lack of musical entertainment for a second. *John* just smiled beneath his mask.

"Who the hell are you?" some drunk wearing a Miller Fall's Volunteer Fire Department t-shirt and sweat-stained *DeRueter Brothers'* Farm cap shouted. A few of his drunken buddies chimed in, laughing and punched each other in response.

"Well, my good man, that is a mighty fine question indeed," *John* shouted and gave the smiling fireman a nod. He stood straight up, put his hands back on his hips, and tilted his head to the side. He threw out his hand toward *Paul* and she frantically fussed with the digital jukebox and the small device she had sitting on a table. A few cracking noises burst through the bar's speakers. *John* shot her a quick glance and just as quickly turned his attention back to the anxious crowd.

"It's too fuckin' late for a band. What are you guys, some kind of comedy act or some shit?" a different drunk cried out, followed by a hoot of laughter and applause.

"Well, it's funny that you should mention that luv," *John* bowed down, his masked nose almost touching his knee, and swiftly stood back up.

"Say, we didn't hire any entertainment tonight, mister," Bessie shouted and leaned against the wet bar. She was getting too old for this and just didn't have the energy anymore. She still had to keep things on the up and up for Jack, the owner. She didn't want any more trouble. She needed this job. When Elmer passed away last winter, it left her without much money and she needed all she could just to pay the lot rent at Happy Pines trailer park. So, here she was, at almost midnight, serving all these annoying drunks and now, these whacked out strangers, whether she wanted to or not.

"Oh, have no fear, my dear; we are strictly, volunteer." *John* chuckled at the unplanned rhyme and waved a wide, sweeping arm toward the stout, elderly bartender. ". . . . and we won't leave your sweet patrons disappointed." The beginning thumping bass lines of *"Obla-Dee-ob-la-da"* pounded out through the bar's cheap speakers. *John* gave *Paul* an approving nod and turned back to the awaiting crowd.

They began cheering, dancing and swaying to the pounding beat. *John* crossed his arms and nodded along with the bass. The drunken mass of bodies merged into one big sea of smiles and flesh as *"Twist and Shout"* came roaring through the speakers. It only enhanced the craziness of the party inside the Torchlight Inn. *John* and the rest of the Fab Four just nodded in anticipation.

As the song ended and the beginning notes of *"The Magical Mystery Tour"* played, *John* held his leather-clad arms wide in a welcoming gesture and lip-synced the song to the excited, swaying crowd. The crowd froze in confusion and shock.

"Roll up, roll up for the mystery tour, step right this way." He sang along as he swiftly flung his trench coat back and brandished the shotgun. The others followed in concert.

"The magical mystery tour is dying to take you away." They all sang and let loose a volley of shots into the drunken, oblivious mass of bodies.

"Take you today," More shots rang out and the

smell of iron and cordite filled the bar. Crimson rain filled the air and met the straining tones of "*I am the Walrus*". *John* stepped toward the crowd of panicked customers and spotted a young girl, barely drinking age, hunched underneath the padded bar rail. He paused, jerked his gaze onto her, and lowered the shotgun. He offered her his gloved hand. She stared wide-eyed and her pale skin was covered in bloody spots. She looked like she had chicken-pox, *John* mused, and tilted his head. He shook his hand at her again and nodded for her to take it. She reached out a trembling, thin hand and wept uncontrollably. He took it gently and helped her up on her wobbly knees. She stared at him in disbelief and shock and he leaned into her and snatched her by the waist. Her tight jeans and white sweater were painted red like a Rorschach test. He whispered in her shaking ear.

"You say hello . . . I say . . . Goodbye!" The young girl's head exploded with a loud splash; turned to a red and fleshy mush, and splattered the Bud Light sign behind the bar. He let her limp body go and it landed with a wet and sickly slap. He stared down at the headless corpse and shrugged his shoulders. The bar was filled with gunshots, smoke and screams of terror. He felt his member growing in his tight, rainbow-colored bell-bottoms as he jumped up onto the bar.

Below, the entire bar was in chaos. His three bandmates were busy, blowing heads and limbs off or slicing gaping holes into the stunned patrons. The floor was slowly being swallowed up by the gallons of blood being spilt from the panicking people of the Torchlight Inn. He smiled beneath his mask and reached full erection. He needed to find her, *but which one was she?* he wondered, surveying the carnage before him.

George had the redneck wearing the *DeRueter* cap deepthroating the Ithaca Deerslayer's barrel as he mockingly thrust his hips at the sobbing farmer. The tears stopped abruptly as the rifle barrel jerked and vomited the hat and it's mass of gristle, bone and blood in a wide pattern into the scrambling crowd behind it. *George* let the glistening shotgun drop to his side and leaned backwards, his face looking up to the white dry-walled ceiling. He let out a bellow of laughter.

Ringo was fighting off three drunks, obviously under-aged drinkers. A tall, lanky fellow punched him in the jaw shifting his mask to the side but he paid no heed and buried his machete into the young man's chest. He buried it so deep, it came poking out the back of his darkly stained Lil'-Wayne t-shirt. The other juvenile assailant was short, stocky with a yellow and black rugby shirt and a backwards ball cap. *Ringo* grasped the punk's throat. He was doing a mighty fine Darth Vader impression, *John* thought and chuckled. The youth punched and kicked at him. The frantic attempts and cries for mercy were met with cold indifference and mocking laughter. All around them was wild and filled with screams and cries of death and pain. *Ringo* stomped his big, booted foot onto the chest of the limp *Lil' Wayne* fan and yanked the machete free, pulling with it a long, stringy, bloody cobweb of flesh and yellow fat. He wiped the thin blade on the limp body of the scrawny drunk and brought his attention back to the flailing teen in his tight grasp.

The young drunk scratched and clawed at *Ringo's* leather sleeve, and desperately kicked at his ribs. Unfortunately for the dangling teen, he was much too short. *John* found that hilarious, let out a howl, brought his hands to his hips again and watched on as *Ringo* brought the machete's tip to the spazzing kid's face. His wide blue eyes seemed to want to burst out from their sockets as the tip of the blade slightly pricked into the soft skin between them. His mouth gaped open wide in a silent plea but he didn't have a chance to utter a word as *Ringo's* forearm muscles tensed, bulged. He thrust the wide blade through the drunken teen's skull. It sank deep, gracefully, as if the flesh and bone was mere Cool Whip. Blood came rushing from the fresh wound and painted *Ringo* in a warm hue of red. He seemed to relish in its warmth. *That boy is one disturbed individual, John* thought and his groin called out to him once again. He grabbed it and tried to make it obey; it fought against its tight polyester constraints and refused to go away. *Now is not the damn time, blast it*, he whispered through gritted teeth and pushed the carnal urge out of his mind. Finding the "One" was the mission and he must stay on task. He needed to finish assessing the situation before engaging in the urge. A shrill shriek blasted off near the dartboards. He jerked his head to find the source. When he found it, his erection grew harder and he smiled wide in satisfaction.

Paul stared at the limp body of a woman, a headless woman at that. In her left hand, she held tightly onto the blood-drenched machete. Long veins of blood and flesh hung from the blade and stretched to the floor where it spilled out and turned the black and white checkers into one solid color — blood red. That wasn't the sight that made *John* smile with pride and his groin swell in ecstasy. It was the fixed, blank stare of the dead woman's severed head in *Paul's* right hand that made him shiver with glee. The red and green Christmas lights caught the glistening, slimy veins as they twitched and splashed in jerky motions from the woman's crudely hewn head. Her mouth hung down, caught in a panicked death scream. Paul slightly swung the head back and forth, like a pendulum. Her laughter grew louder and more intense with every swing of the dead woman's head, as it created an arcing swathe of congealing blood and gristle above the blood-soaked corpse.

"Oh Luv, Edvard Munch would have been oh so proud," he shouted over the loud, distorted guitar of *"Helter Skelter"*.

The chaos reigned about him. *John* smiled and nodded in satisfaction. However, his hard prick called for attention. He reached down, gave it a tug, and adjusted his package. He must find her — the

One. His heart stopped as a crowd of burly men came crashing into the bar from behind the pool table brandishing pistols. However, that wasn't the sight that made *John*'s heart pound or his member salute even higher . . . no, not at all. The ravishing blonde reminded him of Botticelli's *Birth of Venus.* She sat huddled against the video game.

"Ah, there she is." He smiled, grabbing both of his guns as he walked down the bar, towards the fray. As he looked closer at the hysterical girl, he stopped in mid stride. It *was* she. The one they were there for. He realized, and suddenly the blood returned to his brain and he smiled wide beneath the latex mask.

11.

"Everybody's trying to be my baby"

"What the hell was that?" Maurice froze as he lifted a case of Coors Light and turned his head toward the cooler door. His breath sent puffs of white vapor into the cooler's soft yellow glow.

"What? I don't hear anything." Ellen lugged a case of frozen chicken wings from the floor and dropped it on top of a stack of Bud Light cases. She wiped her moist forehead and brushed her raven black hair away from her deep green eyes as she grinned wide, exposing a perfectly white smile and mile deep dimples on her apple cheeks. He couldn't help looking at her large, hard nipples poking through her T-shirt. He tried to ignore them but found himself staring. He blushed. She batted her long eyelashes at him and grabbed a hold of the case of beer he was holding onto. Their hands touched. They were ice cold but Maurice couldn't help but feel himself beginning to sweat. Ellen yanked the case of beer into her hips and leaned into him and kept smiling as she made sure to keep their hypnotizing gaze locked. He swallowed hard and felt his penis press against his Dockers.

This is bad man. Get your ass outta here, Mo, NOW! His consciousness spoke loud and clear but his groin didn't agree and struggled even harder to be free. Ellen yanked the case of beer from his cold grip; it crashed to the concrete floor, and beer began to spread out under their shoes.

"Come on, baby, I've had my eye on you all night. You are wasting your time with that psycho bitch, Ashley. She's not all-there, honey," Ellen's bright eyes sparkled in the glow and her inviting smile drew his attention in.

"Me? Well babe, I just wanna *fuck* you." Her hand sprung forward and found purchase on his swollen crotch. His breath caught in his taut throat. Before he could react, she lunged at him and sunk her moist, pink tongue into his surprised mouth as he fell backwards into the stacks of full kegs.

"Hey, what the hell are you doing?" Maurice protested shoving Ellen away, but she stood fast and her hand didn't let go of his growing member. She lunged at him and tried to unzip his pants. He pulled back and pushed her away. She let go of her grip on his groin and smiled.

"Come on now, you have to know just who your *fiancé* is, don't you?" Ellen asked as she gained her balance and rubbed her already hard nipples. He forced himself to ignore them and focus on what was going on.

"What the hell are you talkin' about?" he asked and stepped back toward the cooler's door.

Then the cooler was filled with the sounds of screams and gunshots.

12.

"Helter Skelter"

The entire bar-room was hell on earth. It was a slaughterhouse with a Liverpool soundtrack. *John* watched on with an aroused smile and compulsively rubbed the protruding bulge in his pants. His target was the thin blonde cowering behind the electronic dartboard. The fear fed his sexual urge. A long drip of drool fell from his gaping mouth and onto his chest. He wiped the spittle from his lips and zeroed in on his prey, his hand never leaving his throbbing package.

"Oh, there she is, there she is," *John* continued cooing as he swung the razor-sharp machete down on top of a man's head. The blade split the Buffalo Bill's ball cap in half. The hat stuck to the blade as *John* kicked the rest of the man's body free. A wide arcing sanguine path followed the limp body as it slid into the screaming crowd, who were fighting to find an exit from the nightmare. They were showered by blood and grey matter and their luck was about to take a turn for the worse.

"Where you lil' rabbits runnin' off to?" *Ringo's* deep voice caught three young men and two girls as they smashed a window with a chair, trying desperately to make their escape. They froze in their tracks and all trembled with fear, blabbering large tears. *Ringo* tilted his head, as a dog would, finding their fear-filled tears fascinating.

The young kid with one leg halfway out the window stopped and grabbed a hold of a short redheaded girl in front of him. His voice cracked as long streams of tears fell from his wide eyes.

"Hey dude, I don't know what the hell you guys want but, hey . . . I . . . Uh," His entire body shook and his head darted back and forth between the behemoth holding the gore covered machete and the trembling girl in front of him. He was struggling with something, *Ringo* could tell, and he felt his malformed lips separate into a surreal smile as the twitchy youngster shoved the frightened girl toward him. *Ringo* laughed as he raised the shotgun and laughed more as the slug shattered the escaping lad's chest. The rest of them cried and begged for mercy. *Ringo* was having none of it. He shoved the shotgun back into the side holster.

"Come here rabbit." He grabbed the redhead girl in a headlock and pulled her into his large body. She just collapsed. He saw a wet spot spreading through her jeans and a pool of yellow piss gathering underneath her. He chuckled and gave her a gentle squeeze.

"Silly rabbit." Large muscles in his arm flexed, almost tore the sleeve; the slack girl's eyes seemed to pop out of their sockets as there was a loud crack. A shard of white vertebrae jabbed out from her neck, followed by warm, bright red blood and a dark brown liquid. It soaked through *Ringo's* jacket and he shook his head in disappointment.

"Stupid rabbit." He threw her limp body down and it slumped to the wet floor. The other kids stared down at their dead friend in horror and disbelief of what was happening all around them. Their bodies refused to move. That pleased *Ringo* and brought a smile back to his distorted face. A loud shotgun blast exploded in his left ear and he fell to one knee in agonizing pain as he felt warm blood shoot from his blasted eardrum. He watched as the other girl in the *Lady GaGa* shirt's entire abdomen disappeared in a burst of blood and ragged flesh.

"Stop toying with them. They aren't your wee pets, you tosser!" *Paul* looked down at the large man and shook her head. He grumbled and stood up, a bit woozy and fought to keep his balance. Once the cute, tweeting birds stopped their singing, he looked about for his next rabbit. He didn't have to look too long as several staggering bar patrons shook with fear and tried to make their way out through the broken window. With a few flashes of the machete's blade, the shards of broken glass were pasted with blood and hanging flesh.

The smell of burnt meat began to fill the room. Gray smoke began to billow out from behind the bar, from the kitchen area. The food's attendant lay dead on the floor. Bessie, the old woman, had a broken Jameson bottle jammed into her throat and her life's blood began to congeal on the yellowing tiled floor underneath the rubber bar mat. *George* stepped onto the rotund woman's stomach, headed back to the smoky kitchen area, and chuckled as he grabbed the spatula and threw the burning hamburgers into the steel sink next to the large cooler. His pink tongue darted out from the mask and licked the hot fat from the spatula and it burned. He paid no heed and turned the corner, heading back around the bar towards the cooler door. Dying to get back into the action.

13.

"What you're doing"

"Ah, come here my precious." *John* hopped down from the bar and approached the terrified blonde who was hiding behind the pool table. She just crunched back and disappeared behind the large machine. A flood of bodies rushed between them, including Scooter. He saw the tall, masked man making his way toward the dartboard. He caught a glimpse of Ashley's long blonde hair. *No fuckin' way*, he thought, and he pulled out his Buck knife and shoved Sacks out of the way. He forced his way through the panicked crowd.

A flurry of blows sent many frantic bar-goers tumbling and stumbling as *John* shot and disemboweled them along the path to his target. His treadless boots slipped on the blood and urine as he made his way to the blonde. He was focused and didn't even notice the lanky form rushing toward him from off to his right. He lost his breath as he was smashed into the Svedka Vodka sign hanging from the opposite wall. The neon sign exploded, sending shards of glass and metal flying. *John* felt the jagged glass penetrated the left side of his mask and puncture his skin. One piece barely missed slicing into his eye and blinding him. He fought to gain his balance and the lanky man brought down the knife toward his chest.

John sidestepped the blade and it continued and lodged inside the dark wooden wall. He jammed the heel of his boot into the side of the tall man's knee and it made a sickly crunch and then gave way. Scooter crashed to the floor, grasping his knee in agony.

"Motherfucker, I'm gonna gut you like a—"

"Tsk, Tsk, my good man." *John* knelt down and grabbed Scooter's scruffy chin. "Don't be a big blue meanie, for it will be I who will be doing the gutting this fine evening."

He smiled and brought the dripping machete up to Scooter's throat, in a slow, mocking motion.

The over-dramatic gesture gave Ashley the

opportunity to make a break for it. She slowly, very cautiously, stood up from behind the dartboard and ran for the deck that was still full of screaming people and total chaos. She almost made it to the corner of the pool table when *Paul's* small but lithe frame jumped in her way. Blocking her escape.

"Where might you be scurrying off to, my sweet?" *Paul* quizzed, with one hand on her hip and the other shoving the shotgun in her face.

"I . . . uh . . . p-l-e-a-s-s, don't . . . " Ashley cried and held her shaking hands to her face.

"Is this the one?" *Paul* called to *John*, who was busy toying with Scooter's busted up knee. She didn't look away. She held the sawn-off shotgun perfectly motionless. A dead bead on Ashley's quivering head.

"Aye, she be the one," *John* said. His tone was filled with hate, laughter, and lust, all rolled up in a tight, five word response. *Paul* always loved it when he spoke to her like that.

"She matches the photo and the paperwork checks out," he finished as he stood up.

"Get the fuck away from her you bitch," Scooter screamed through the pain that was ravaging his shattered knee.

"Well, well, well. Look at the spunk in you, mate." *John*'s voice rose and he shook his head in approval. He dropped the slimy blade to his side and lifted the shotgun to Scooter's anguished face. He pulled the trigger. Scooter's entire head disappeared. Large pieces of ripped flesh, shattered bone and grey matter splattered the Miller Lite 2010 NASCAR schedule poster on the wall behind him. The smell of cordite and blood made his erection harder.

"I hate spunk."

He sheathed the machete as the din of death and chaos reigned inside the rest of the bar. *Ringo* and *George* were doing their pre-set tasks and laying waste to the entire occupants of the Torchlight Inn. The dreadful cries and pleas for mercy were being answered with the loud clamoring of shotgun blasts or the sick slap of steel on flesh. Those heavenly sounds made *John* a very happy, happy man. The meat inside his trousers twitched with compiling excitement.

14.

"Help"

"Get down," Maurice whispered and pointed toward the old floor of the cooler. The red and green Christmas lights broke the dim light of the cooler; with it came the sounds of gunfire. It seemed, to him, like a slaughterhouse out in the bar-room. The cries of fear and the baying of the dying filled the small room. Maurice's hair stood up on the back of his neck and forearms. He knew that sound all too well and could feel the adrenaline and endorphins beginning to kick in and course their way through his entire body.

He shoved Ellen down onto the floor and followed her. He scanned the area for anything useful. He didn't have a clue as to what was going on out there but he knew the gruesome sound and smell of death that was beginning to fill the cooler. He let out a small disappointed breath when he couldn't find anything. Ellen just looked up at him with her big, wide brown doe-eyes that just cried out of help. He took a deep breath and gently opened up a case of beer and slowly took out a bottle and held it like a knife. He crouched down and waited.

They stared in confusion as the metallic clunk of the cooler door's latch broke the heavy silence.

The heavy door closed slowly and the din from hell went with it. Maurice could hear the padding of heavy feet and heavy breathing as it grew closer. He held the bottle ready to strike. He could feel his sweat freezing as it rolled down his face and body. His muscles tensed as the form came around the rack full of cases of beer. He brought the bottle down onto the head of the figure as it rounded the corner. It let out a shrill, girlish cry as the bottle smashed. Whoever it was staggered backwards, grabbing their head.

"What the *fuc* . . . " Sackett – *Sacks* — belted as he fell to his knees amidst brown shards of broken glass and beer foam.

Maurice grabbed the large man and pulled him

behind the safety of the large stacks of beer. He tried to brush away the beer bottle pieces.

"Man, I'm sorry, what the hell is going *on* out there?" he asked. He tried to hide his fear, and thought for sure it didn't work.

"Ah, shit . . . ya busted my goddamn noggin', man," Sackett whimpered and rubbed his head. He took his soaked ball cap off and shook it. He leaned against the wall of beer cases and tried to catch his breath.

"Sorry, sorry. Calm down and tell me what's going on?" Maurice grabbed him by his shoulders and shook him.

"I . . . dunno, man . . . these crazy fuckers came in 'n started playin' some weird 60's music and shit, 'n started shooting and cutting shit up," Sackett began to cry.

"For no *reason*?" Ellen chimed in. She leaned closer and wiped the beer and glass shards from Sackett's trembling head.

"I just told you . . . I don't know what the hell they want." Sackett's tears came down faster and stronger. He cupped his chubby cheeks in his hands and his entire body shook. Maurice knew it was from shock and knew that he wasn't going to get any more useful information from him. He looked about, frantically, but didn't know what for. Any brilliant answer wasn't forthcoming and he knew it.

Ellen cleaned the glass out of Sackett's hair and tried to dry him off with the bar towel that she kept tucked into her tight jeans.

"Okay . . . okay . . . do you have any weapons on you?" Maurice asked.

"I, uh, um . . . I ..." Sackett fumbled and looked about confused.

"Ya know . . . a gun or a goddamn knife?" Maurice grabbed Sackett's jiggling face and forced his gaze onto him. His fat cheeks were pinched and his lips made an over-exaggerated fish-lips face. His large eyes were wide and the pupils were dilated.

"Uh . . . yeah, I . . . think so," He fumbled around his waist and let out a giggle as he pulled out the biggest knife Maurice had ever seen. He had seen far too many blades in his short years.

"Nice." Maurice took the Bowie knife from Sackett's beer- and sweat-covered face, and gently patted him on the cheeks. "Now we have something."

"What are we going to do?" Ellen yanked on

Maurice's shoulder, nearly knocking him over.

He caught his balance and shot her a cold look.

"We don't know what's going on out there, and *his* drunken ass isn't going to help us at all," he said pointing to Sackett.

"A bunch of crazy, fuck . . . " Sackett's words flitted off into the cold air of the cooler. The yellow light flickered and the muffled shouts and screams still penetrated their icy prison. Maurice knew he needed to do something and fast. It was damn cold and his muscles had started to tighten up. He stared at the large blade and it caught the flickering light in its reflection, He could see his own panicked eyes staring back at him.

He put his ear against the cold door and didn't have to strain to hear the carnage raging beyond it.

15.

"Do you want to know a secret?"

"Well hello, Love," *John* said and swaggered toward Ashley.

"Wh-ooo . . . *are* y-ooou?" she squeaked, struggling against *Paul's* strong grip on her hair. Her wide brown eyes flickered with tears and refracted the myriad of Christmas lights strung haphazardly about the bar's ceiling and walls.

"Oh, no, no, no. The more important question for this fine wintry evening is," he jumped in close to her face and gently lifted a long strand of her blonde hair and sniffed it, then let it fly freely back down to her quivering shoulder. *Paul* released her and stepped back, letting her leader take control.

"Who YOU are?" He suddenly snatched the tumbling golden hair and yanked her head into his chest and staring deep into her crying eyes, he laughed.

"You have two seconds to let her go boy, or I'm gonna wipe the goddamned floor with all your sorry asses." Daddy's booming voice startled *John* and he jumped back, but kept a strong grip on the screaming girl's golden locks.

Behind Daddy came five or six large men, all wielding pistols of various sizes and calibers. Their intent was obvious and *John's* erection returned, twitched, and looked forward to finally having a challenge. He yanked Ashley in front of him, hiding behind her. He stepped backwards toward the bar, and he was happy.

"Well, well, welcome to the show, gentlemen," *John* mocked and pulled Ashley closer to him. He jammed the barrel of the shotgun into her quivering mouth, shattering teeth and slicing her pink gums wide open, Blood poured out of her mouth, ran down the barrel, and covered her chin and the front of her shirt. She cried out in pain.

He smiled. "Step right this way."

"Oh, I'll be doin' some steppin' alright, you pecker-head sumbitch. I'll be steppin' a mud hole in your scrawny, freak ass," Daddy screamed, and ran toward *John*. One of the large men behind him grabbed his tensed arm and yanked him back as *John* shoved the barrel of the sawn-off shotgun deeper into Ashley's bloody mouth. Her muffled scream and the man's strong grip caused the old farmer to halt in his tracks.

A blast of gunfire took out the pool table light and sent sparks, metallic shrapnel and plastic flying. *George* stood against the wall next to the pool table, his shotgun smoking from the blast. The rest of the men scrambled backward towards the double doors of the outdoor deck of the bar. Splinters of wood filled the air as they took cover.

"Boy, *George*, what a bloody good shot," *John* said and yanked Ashley backward, making sure to run her breast against his raging hard on.

"Why thank you, good sir," *George* nodded and cocked the shotgun, sending the empty shell casing bouncing off the wall and onto the slick, gore-covered floor.

"And, for my next trick," *George* teased and fired three rounds into the wall next to the door of the deck. A loud groan blasted back, answering the call of the shotgun blast. A short, scrawny man stumbled into the doorway, holding his stomach. A large red stain appeared and was rapidly spreading like a napkin soaking up a nice red wine. The gaunt man's face turned pale and he fell to his knees in the center of the double doors. *George* took aim and made sure the dying man didn't suffer. It looked as though a crimson colored watermelon erupted in one single burst. The man's face and head disappeared into the darkness of the makeshift room. Screams of horror and anger made the shredded body, collapsing onto the floor, inaudible. *George* chuckled and reloaded.

"What's the matter, lads? Don't have enough stones to come out and play?" *John* teased, gyrated his polyester covered hips against Ashley's shaking rear end. She tried to scream but the high-pitched cry for help was lost amongst the din of all the dying, gunshots and the haunting sounds of "*With a little help from my friends*".

"I'm gonna fuck your world up, you piece of shit," Daddy screamed. His voice full of rage could be heard over the chaos and music. *John* just let out a belly laugh and motioned with his head toward *Ringo*.

"Some cover would be lovely, if you please," He looked at the overturned table behind *Ringo*. The big man yanked his machete free from a struggling grizzled farmer and the old man's slimy intestines came with it. He flicked the blade, trying to free it from the sausage-like mass, but it clung to it, as if it were glued. He repeatedly shook the blade but the bloody tube just kept coming out of the dying man, like some horrific magic trick gone wrong.

"'Allo. Would you mind stopping all that shite and get that bloody table over here," *John's* voice held no humor or appreciation for the comical scene the big lummox was displaying in front of him.

"Right," *Ringo* hung his head and his broad shoulders slumped as he yanked the remaining bloody intestines free from the machete and sheathed it in its place on his wide leather belt. He then hurriedly snatched the table up and ran to where *John* stood, tapping his foot. He set the table down and knelt behind it. His large frame barely fit behind the large bar table. *John* shook his head and yanked the flailing girl to the bar's sticky floor.

"Stay here Crumpet," *John* said. He took a black plastic zip-tie, yanked her hands to the tarnished brass foot railing of the bar, and secured her. She cried out as the plastic sliced deep into her thin wrists and blood ran down and joined the thick layer of crimson already covering the floor. *John* ignored her, picked up the shotgun from the gore on floor, and wiped it on Ashley's heaving back as she wretched. He kicked her in the ribs and she let a large woof of air and collapsed, landing with a splash on the wet floor.

"Alright, fellows, let's give these buggers an early Happy Christmas gift." *John* aimed from his squat position behind the table and fired into the doorway of the deck. The others followed suit.

The small bar once again filled with smoke and the smell of cordite, sweat and panic. The Fearsome Four all let out a collective laugh. It echoed all the way into the cooler. Somehow, the chilling laughter was colder.

16.

"I'll get you"

"You motherfuckers are done," Daddy said through gritted, chew-stained teeth. "I swear to Christ, I will skull-fuck you *all*." He double checked the bullets in his nickel plated Smith & Wesson 29 and slammed the cylinder shut with satisfaction. He spat a wad of brackish chunks on the red soaked floor. He looked across the doorway at the remaining partygoers and tried to assess the situation. He counted four armed freaks in and around the bar, but wasn't sure if there were more somewhere else killing his friends and family. Surely all the tough as nails farmers and jocks would have stormed them if there were only two. Or so he'd hoped. Who *knew* anymore with the pussified world we all lived in? he grumbled. He stared down at the bloody mess that was once Butch VanLaken. His body still twitched and nerves kicked his leg out like it was starting his old *Harley*. Daddy's grasp grew tighter on the walnut grip of his monster pistol. He had two men behind him. Ronnie Cauwels and Sammy Sizemore; both worked on his farm and were damn hard working men. He wasn't so sure about fighting with guns and killing. He didn't have time to worry about that shit. He looked at them and Ronnie was looking pissed and ready for bear. Sammy, on the other hand, looked like he was just nailed in the ass by his prize winning bull. That, and Daddy noticed the puddle growing under the chubby man's feet. He shook his head in disgust and focused on Ronnie, whose large brown eyes seemed to want to burst. A huge blue vein popped out of his forehead and throbbed at his temple. His thin upper-lip twitched. Daddy smiled at that. He knew the scrawny scrapper would have his back. He held up his pistol and pointed at the cylinder.

"Double-check your ammo, boys," he whispered and turned back toward the fidgeting figures across the doorway. The smell of gunpowder filled the room. He made the same motion to the four men fighting for hiding space alongside the other wall.

They fiddled about with their pistols and he hoped they understood what he meant. His friends were good folks, but some of them were dumber than Bachman's bitch, who swam across the river to get a drink of water. Nevertheless, his daughter was in deep shit and he didn't have time to deal or worry about them. He took a deep breath, held up three fingers to the other group and brought them down as he mouthed the countdown.

Two…Three…

"Die, you sick *fuck* . . . " Daddy bellowed as he turned the corner and let loose a volley of shots from his hand-cannon. The others followed behind the big man. Guns a-blazing.

17.

"Wait"

"Sounds like the damn streets of Durham out there. What the hell is going on?" Maurice said, with his ear pressed against the frost-covered metal door of the cooler. He turned back toward Ellen and Sackett, who was dabbing his wounded head.

"Alright, I'm going out there. You guys can do whatever you want. But my fiancé is in the middle of all that shit and she needs me." Maurice forced the words out and took a deep breath.

"I don't think that's such a good idea," Ellen said, grabbing his arm tightly and trying to pull him away from the door. He resisted and broke free.

"Screw that, she needs me, goddammit," He glared at her and she backed away, hitting the large stacks.

"I'm goin' with ya." Sackett looked up, tossed the bloody rag to the floor and reached behind his back. He pulled out a Glock 45 and held it up, smiling.

"Where the hell did you get that?" Maurice stared at him in disbelief.

"Ya didn't think I was gonna give this baby to you did ya? I may be dumb, but I ain't *stupid*," he laughed with a snort and kissed the flat black barrel.

"Well . . . just don't shoot me in the back okay?" Maurice ordered, shaking his head.

"You got it, chief." Sackett winked, gripped the pistol with both hands and readied himself behind Maurice. He could see Sackett trembling and still managing to sweat inside a 38 degree cooler.

"Ellen, you stay here and keep trying to get a signal and if you *do* get one, fucking call 911, got it?" Maurice nodded at her and he turned and gripped the cold metal door handle.

"Yeah, but I don't think it's gonna work in here." Her voice was soft, almost a whisper. Maurice didn't even notice or care. The love of his life was out there in the slaughterhouse, and she needed him. He took a deep breath, pulled the long handle toward him, and shoved the heavy door open.

18.

"Twist and Shout"

Daddy's first shot from the long-barreled pistol caught *George* in the hand and it turned every finger into a bloody mush; his shotgun fell to the floor. Daddy smiled and let loose another shot. It splintered the wood next to *George*'s stunned head. Sharp splinters of wood were sprayed into the air and *George* ducked for cover behind the corner of the wall. Again, Daddy smiled and jumped behind the pool table.

"Come get some motherfuckers," Daddy shouted and peeked over the felt top of the pool table. He could see one form behind an upturned table and the blood splatter on the wall where his first shot had found a home. He liked the sight of blood and smell of gunpowder. He waited to see what other dumb bastard reared his ugly head so he could blow it off. His little baby was hurt and he wasn't about to let anything more happen to the last precious thing he had on this planet. He breathed deep; he could feel his heart race.

"Die," Ronnie yelled and let loose with random shots that tore into the bar and shattered several bottles of vodka and whiskey. All three shots missed their mark and left him exposed in the middle of the pool room. *John* chuckled as he pulled the trigger. A bright muzzle flash filled the small room and a pixelated red mist exited Ronnie's back; his bulging eyes just stared forward, not focusing on anything as he dropped to his knees in a heap. Part of his lung hung out through the back of his leather vest and Daddy did all he could do to keep from puking up the night's consumption of beer and whiskey. It didn't work and he let loose a stream of brown- and yellow-colored vomit that splattered against the dark walls. He wiped his mouth and watched his friend's lifeblood slowly spread across the white and black checkerboard floor. He tightened his grip on the Smith & Wesson and spat on the floor. The dark brown spittle mixed with the deep red of Ronnie's blood and turned to a brackish clump. Daddy felt bile rise in his burning throat and managed to hold back the next round of puke.

"That's one down mate. Who's next?" *John* laughed as Ronnie let out a death rattle and slid to the floor, his large eyes fixed on Daddy, who swallowed hard and prayed for the first time in years.

"Get in here you goddamn pussies!" Daddy bellowed to the men hiding in the shadows of the deck. He heard low whimpers and sobbing. That was the only noise coming from the dark room. He prayed harder.

"I'm guessing you want this precious naughty bit of crumpet that I have. Is that correct mate?" *John* taunted and winked back at Ashley's unmoving form on the bar floor.

"You piece of shit. I will *kill* you if you harm one hair on her head," Daddy scowled and looked over the top of the pool table.

"Oh, bother, I've already done more than harm her hair, lad. She may need some major dental work, but trust me, she will have bigger concerns than her pearly whites by the time this night is over, I'm afraid." *John's* jovial tone dropped and became sombre. He looked back at Ashley's limp form and ejected the spent shell. It ricocheted off the table and landed on the slick floor.

Daddy's chest felt like it was being crushed between two eighteen-wheelers and his left arm started to tingle. His breath left him and sweat oozed from every pore and soaked through his already wet clothes. He was all too familiar with these symptoms. It wasn't his first ride on this bull. His shaky hand fought with the flap of his shirt pocket and he yanked it off in frustration and desperation. He shoved his sweat-covered hand inside, pulled out a hand full of small white pills, and jammed them into his mouth. He swallowed hard, took a deep breath and let it out. He sprang up fast, brought the large pistol with him, and aimed toward the sound of the Brit's voice.

As he reached his full height and brought the handgun down, he jumped back as the far end of the pool table quickly rose up and rushed toward him. He back-pedaled and smashed into the wall behind him. The large table came down on him in a flash. The small room filled with grunting and laughter as Daddy was pinned against the wall and couldn't move. He knew he was screwed.

"Shall I make a pancake out of 'um, *John*?" *Ringo* huffed, his muscles flexed as he shoved the heavy pool table against the wall. "I want to see his squishes come out, like that last mission in Memphis." *Ringo* giggled and looked at *John* for approval.

"Certainly lad, let's see what comes out of him if you squeeze really hard," *John* said. "But, go much slower this time."

"Aye, Mr. *John.*" *Ringo* flexed his large arms and began to slowly push the pool table. Loud screeching sounds ushered forth as the metal from the sides of the table dug into the linoleum floor. Daddy realized that the trouble he had had breathing a few moments ago was nothing compared to what was a-coming.

19.

"Happiness is a warm gun"

Maurice Ware had been witness to many horrifying things in his young life. Growing up in the violent, gang-banging streets of Durham paled in comparisons to what lay before him as he slowly cracked open the cooler door. What he saw caused his mind and soul to pause with fear and disbelief. He felt the heavy body of Sackett behind him and shoved the large redneck backward.

"What the hell's goin' on, man?" Sackett asked and hopped up and down, trying to see anything through the small opening.

"Shut up," Maurice ordered, shoving the big man backwards. He turned his attention back toward the smoky haze of the dimly lit bar room. He staggered back into Ellen, knocking her to the cold floor.

"Watch it, lard-ass." She shot him a *look* and staggered back to her feet.

"Sorry Ell, I . . . I didn't mean . . . " Sackett's round cheeks flushed and he stared at the floor.

"Knock that shit off, both of you," Maurice hissed, never taking his eyes off the gore on the other side of the door. "There's some seriously messed up shit going on out there . . . " His words trailed off and he fought to inhale. The time to act was *now*. He looked back at Ellen and Sackett and reached out his shaking hand.

"Give me the gun, Sackett. I don't trust your dumb ass." His face illustrated to Sackett that it wasn't really a question.

"Fuck that noise, boss." Sackett shook his head, his jowls jiggled and trailed behind the rest of his rotund head. "This is my baby, and you ain't gonna have it. No way boss." He shuffled his large booted feet in defiance and pulled the gun away from Maurice, still shaking his head: *no*.

"Ah, the hell with this shit," Maurice said. He gripped the handle tighter and did the same with the large knife in his other hand. "Let's go." He shoved the large door open slowly, and kept low. He motioned for Sackett to follow him. He did as he was ordered and, with a smug grin on his face, held the pistol out in front of him parallel to the ground, just like they do in the movies. Maurice shook his head in frustration.

He could only open the cooler door a couple of feet when it was met with resistance. He tried to push it open, and when he did, a large form fell down in front of him, blocking the entrance. A rusty and bitter smell assaulted his nostrils as he squatted down to examine the body. His eyes darted to the motion beyond the door, and the sounds of metal screeching and digging into something metallic and shrill made him cringe. He hoped he wasn't noticed and nervously turned his attention to the body blocking the doorway.

He grabbed what he thought was the shoulder of a male and the body was soaked with some liquid. It was warm and slimy, like the skin that forms on the top of the warm pudding his mother used to make for him when he wasn't feeling well. The rubbery substance stuck to his hand and with it came the putrid smell of feces and second-time whisky. He felt bile rush up into his mouth and he forced himself to swallow.

"Come on boss, let's go kick some freak ass."

Sackett's' clumsy attempt at whispering made Maurice shudder.

"Shut the fuck up, you idiot." Maurice let go of the slimy body and tried to flick the goo from his hand. It refused to let go. He fought back more bile and stood up. He looked out into the bar, could only see the pool table up in one end. A big monster of a man in a long leather trench coat was pushing the table. The long black trench coat was coated in a slick shiny film of what Maurice thought was blood. More vomit fought to be released. He belched.

"What the hell we waitin' for, boss?" Sackett's shaky voice broke Maurice's gaze at the blood-slathered man and he turned to face him

"It's worse than I thought. You really need to give me that gun, and I'm fixin' to knock your Podunk ass out to get it." Maurice snatched the gun from Sackett's sweaty hands. "They are some bad mothers out there, man. This isn't some damn turkey shoot." He wiped his goo-slathered hand on Sackett's t-shirt and turned his attention back to the scene outside the cooler. "No turkey shoot at all." He stepped over the bloody corpse and ducked behind the bar, not really knowing what to do next.

20.

"Ask me why"

"Feeling a bit cramped are ya, tough guy?" *John* quipped as he left the safe confines of the upturned table.

"*Paul, George*, finish up with them and take care of the wankers tossing off out there," *John* shouted and pointed his shotgun at the opening to the outdoor deck. He hoped some fool would pop their head around the corner. He could hear the big redneck fighting to breathe under the pressure of the pool table and the crushing strength of *Ringo*. It made him smile. It was a good night for smiling.

"Fuck off and die, asshole," Daddy threatened as best he could between the wall and pool table.

"Now, now, good sir. One should not be threatening anyone in your, um . . . position." *John* chortled through the mask, tasting the anger in the trapped man's eyes. It permeated the death-filled air and it gave him stirrings. Again, he smiled.

"I don't give a flyin' fuck in rollin' donut asshole, if you hurt my daughter, I'll *KILL YOU!*" Blood flew from his smothered mouth and his words rang funny, like a little child, whose cheeks were being squeezed by an annoying aunt.

George and *Paul* rushed to *John*'s side, raised their shotguns, and slowly approached the darkened outdoor deck. *George* wrapped a bar towel around his mangled hand. Bright red blood immediately soaked through it. He still favored the flesh mound of a hand and, resting the shotgun in the crook of his elbow, he followed *Paul*.

"Make it quick, we have business to tend to, if you please." *John*'s tone was playful, yet focused. He was more than pleased when the blue tarped room lit up with a flurry of muzzle flashes and cries for mercy and pain. It was like visceral and auditory Viagra for him. He relished in it.

"Why the hell are you doin' this, you piece of shit?" Daddy forced the words out and more blood trickled from the corner of his mashed face.

"*Why*, you ask?" *John* stepped close and leaned into the big man's flushed, purple and pink face. "That's a fair question." He leaned against the wall and put his hand on the man's shoulder. "It is your daughter. She is the reason why you all have to die tonight," John whispered into Daddy's ear. A small droplet of deep, red blood ran from his inner ear and fell onto his bib overalls.

"My . . . *daughter?* Ashley Girl? WH . . . *Why?*" Daddy's body went slack and a lone tear glistened in his eye and rolled down his bruised cheek, mixing with the blood running from his ear. The pool table was slowly crushing and cracking each rib. He let out a small whimper. *Ringo* didn't let up the pressure.

"She . . . What did she . . . *do?*" Daddy's words came out in a low hush and his head bobbed back and forth; *John* could tell he was about to lose consciousness. "You leave her . . . alone . . . I gonna . . . kill . . . " His words grew softer and his body went slack.

"Stop," *John* held his hand up to *Ringo* and the big man did as he was told.

"Oh dear, dear Big Daddy." *John* shook his head and patted the waning man's red cheek. "You see, your precious *Ashley Girl,* isn't so innocent." He reached inside his leather trench coat and pulled out a folded sheet of paper; he leaned the shotgun against the blood soaked wall.

"Wha . . . ar . . . yo . . . talkin'—"

"You and I both know that your sweet little lass isn't *yours*, don't we?" *John*'s mask touched the side of Daddy's swollen and bloodied face. He unfolded the paper and shoved it into the wavering man's face. He mumbled incoherently.

"No, she is not a Vanslycke at all, is she?" *John* said, pointing to the paper. "You *can* read can't you Daddy?" *John* teased. "Well then, you can see that this is a birth certificate, correct?" *John* pressed the paper into the Daddy's slack face. "Well this is proof that your *oh so darling* girl, lying over there in a bloody pile, isn't your flesh and blood and this other document is her adoption papers," He pulled the man's head up with yank of his hair. "And on this document, it says where she came from and her *REAL* last name," *John* said. "You remember who she was don't you? You do *remember* her real last name Big Daddy?" *His* voice rose in timbre and volume. *Paul* and *George* returned, covered head to toe in blood. The deck behind them lay in a haunting silence.

"See, it's that little fact that led us here tonight my dying friend," *John* continued. "You see, we have a mission, well, a campaign really." He looked back at the others and waved his hand in a sweeping motion toward them. "And you and her, well, and the rest of you backwater sods have to pay the price.

"Do you know what date it is today? Hmmm?" *John* said. He feigned waiting for a response that he knew wouldn't be forthcoming. "I didn't think so, but considering the bloodline of your beaten sweetness over there, you would think you'd be aware of what a significant day today is." He leaned in and dropped the papers to the floor, where they stuck to the mucky surface and red splotches slowly appeared through them.

"Today is December 8th my good man, and do you know what happened on that date and why your little precious is going to be slaughtered tonight?" *John* straightened and snatched up his shotgun. "Still not ringing any bells for you?" *John* said and walked slowly back toward Ashley's prone body. "The brilliance of John Lennon was snuffed out of existence on this date, Big Daddy, and in case the lack of oxygen to that already small brain of yours still isn't making the connection, let me make it easy for you." He lowered the shotgun into Ashley's slowly rising belly and turned his gaze back to Daddy, who slowly raised his head in protest.

"On the bloody document her name wasn't Ashley Vanslycke. It was Julia. Julia *Chapman*." He shoved the barrel deep into the girl's limp body until blood bubbled up and pooled around the steel. "She was next on the list of Mark David Chapman family members. And I applaud their efforts, and yours of course, in trying to hide and bury that dark fact. It took many hours of research and we've left a pretty long, bloody trail on our way to find her." He looked back up at Daddy, whose burning stare could cut *John* into pieces.

"But, alas, the Chapman line ends here . . . It ends tonight."

The shotgun blast obliterated the tense air and disintegrated the girl's abdomen. Large chunks of bloody flesh, yellow fat and pieces of intestines, liver and lungs filled the air and splattered against the old oak bar. What seemed like an ocean of blood poured out from her gaping wound and set to covering the small pool-room floor.

"*Ringo*, finish him," *John* ordered and shoved the shotgun into the holster on his back. He reached inside the jacket and pulled out the machete.

"We have work to do gents."

21.

"You're gonna lose that girl"

"NO!" Maurice fell to the floor behind the bar as the shotgun went off. His ears rang and his eyes saw white flashes as pain filled his head. He shook his head to clear the concussive stun. He didn't know what it was but his gut told him something bad just happened. Almost as if he himself was shot. He looked around as he lay there and found himself lying right next to the bloody remains of the old lady bartender. Her vacant stare peered right into his. Caked blood covered her entire face and he realized he was lying in the rest of her blood; the slick liquid began to seep into his clothes. It was then that his breath left him. Sackett had fallen on top of him, nearly crushing his ribs as he fell.

"Get the hell off me," he whispered and wheezed. He shoved the big man off and slowly crouched.

"Sorry boss. Sorry." Sackett rolled to one side and rose to one knee next to him. He looked at the old dead woman, and Maurice thought the fat kid was going to cry or puke. Maybe both. He looked around for something, anything, to help him. He thought he heard the sound of sawing, or cutting. Like something he used to hear at the local butchers' shop his uncle ran back in Durham. His stomach turned again and something inside him knew it wasn't good. He didn't think, he didn't fear, he just sprang up, holding the pistol in front of him with two hands and prepared to fire at anything that moved.

When he stood up, he saw the carnage and it made his soul weep. He prayed to God and hoped he was listening, but something told him that all the dead and dying souls inside this small bar already had Him busy. He saw a big muscle-bound man in black leather, pushing an upturned pool table into the wall. His heart skipped as he realized it was Daddy being crushed between the table and the bar's wall. Blood covered the floor, and the Christmas lights created ghastly reflections in the sanguine pool. Two other leather clad figures stood in the yellow light of the bar lights. He didn't have much time to analyze but he could swear that they wear wearing Beatles masks — they *were*. *George*, *Paul* and *Ringo* . . . It was *them*. However, if they were there, where was *John*? he asked as his hands trembled at the surreal scene playing out before him.

"Drop your fucking guns!" Maurice found himself shouting. He saw *George* drop to one knee and raise a shotgun at him. He pulled the trigger. The gun roared in his hands, and the bullets found a home in the mouth of the figure wearing the *George* mask. Blood and skull fragments exploded out the back of his head. The shotgun dropped to the floor as the limp body quickly followed. Maurice pivoted and saw the small figure donned in the *Paul McCartney* mask raise a shotgun and fire. He ducked down behind the bar in time, but Sackett wasn't so lucky. The slug tore into his barrel chest and sent his heart and lungs splashing against the top-shelf liquor behind him. His eyes bulged and he dropped the big knife to the floor, then he collapsed in a heap next to Maurice.

"Oh, now it looks like we have a *live* one mates," a lilting voice said from the other side of the bar.

Maurice leaned over and snagged the knife and shoved it into his belt. He stared up at the top of the bar, just waiting.

He couldn't believe what was happening. This was supposed to be a good trip. A time to celebrate his engagement to the most amazing woman he'd ever met. Yet, here he was, lying in a pool of blood, surrounded by dead people with some kind of psychotic Beatles tribute-band brandishing shotguns like machetes. *What the fuck?* were the words that kept repeating in his flurrying mind. Then the image of Ashley came rushing back to him and his heart about shattered into a million pieces. Where was she and was she okay? He was filled with fear at the possible answers to those questions.

"Come on out and play. You have one of ours and we took one of yours," the voice called, and it sounded close . . . *very* close. "You see, hero. No one gets out of here alive."

Maurice got to his knees and made his way to the swinging bar top. He looked up and saw the reflection of the freaks in the Labatt's Blue beer mirror on the wall above the taps. He needed to do this just right. He tried to force the image of

Ashley, lying dead amongst all the other slaughtered patrons of the Torchlight Inn, from his mind, but the pain in his chest was far worse than any bullet or machete could inflict. He would take as many of those sorry ass freaks out as he could before they got him. He had thought he left the violent "thug" life behind on the dirty streets in North Carolina. He was wrong. He squeezed the grip on the Glock. He decided to check Sackett's pockets for ammunition. He felt sadness engulf him as he rifled through the dead fat man's pockets. Tears filled his eyes as he found two full clips tucked inside the big man's back pocket.

"Thanks, buddy," he whispered, shoving the clips into his front pants pocket. He made his way to the swinging bar top.

"You might as well make it easy, sport, and surrender. You're as good as dead anyway so let's cut to the chase, pardon the pun." The voice chortled and the remaining *Beatles* joined in. The sound of sawing and cutting continued. Maurice's stomach ached and wanted to expel the night's consumption. He fought it back down and decided to act.

When he flipped the heavy bar top open, dove

into the pool table room, and crashed into the pinball machine, Maurice couldn't believe his eyes. He slid on the slick, blood-covered floor. Before him knelt a slim figure in a long leather trench coat with a machete in one hand and a blue Jean clad leg in the other. Ragged flesh and nerves dangled from it and blood poured out, adding to the quarts already covering the entire room.

John turned toward Maurice, chucked the dismembered limb at him, and sprang. The bloody stump caught Maurice in the shoulder and he spun backwards. He tried to right himself but *John* was upon him. Maurice fired the gun and it tore into the charging *Beatle,* who pin-wheeled backward.

Maurice fought to get to his feet and took cover behind the pinball machine.

"A load of bollocks you are, lad. Excellent shot." The wounded *John* dabbed his shoulder and nodded in approval.

"Stay back, you sick fuck!" Maurice shouted and aimed the pistol at the wounded Beatle.

"Let me at 'em, Mr. *John,*" the large mammoth of a man growled and stepped forward. The wounded Lennon held his hand up, stopping the oaf in his tracks.

"No . . . He's *mine*," he said and jerked the blood and sinew from the blade of his machete and slowly approached Maurice.

"Come get some, bitch," Maurice said and aimed the pistol at *John*'s chest. He looked down where *John* was standing; something caught his attention, something familiar. The body on the floor, the one the sick fuck was dismembering was wearing clothes that he recognized. He caught a glimpse of something shining in the light. It was a ring. It was Ash's. It hit him like a Mack truck. "Ashley . . . " A searing pain awoke him from his momentary paralysis and he reached for his side. *John* stood before him with fresh, bright red blood dripping from his blade. Maurice looked down and saw his side was sliced clean open and fresh blood spilled down his leg and onto the floor. He could see the raw meat and yellow-colored fat hanging loose. Once again, white flashes ruled his vision. He staggered backward and grabbed at the wound in his side. His left side went numb and the pistol clunked to the floor. His eyes flashed with white and sharp pinpricks of pain punctured his side. He staggered backward into the *Lord of the Rings* Pinball Machine. It dinged and some ominous voice spoke from it. Maurice's hearing became muddled.

"Was that Chapman bitch yours?" *John* said and slowly approached Maurice. He twirled the long blade like a baton and tilted his masked head as he closed in.

"*Chapman* . . . Wha . . . what? I don't know what the hell you're *talkin'* about," Maurice shouted and forced himself to stand up straight.

"It's no matter. They all had to pay the price. We are here to right the wrongs that this world has chosen to ignore." *John* raised the machete.

Maurice bared his teeth and charged, knocking him to the floor. His mind raced and the tears blinded him. *She's dead*, he kept repeating in his mind. His sorrow was cut short, as *John* grabbed him by the throat and squeezed. He could hear laughter from off to his left. The other two Beatle assholes must be really enjoying this insanity. He landed a punch to the masked man's face and blood flew out from the mouth hole.

"C'mon, Mister *John*, let me at 'em!" Maurice heard the big man beg. It made him smile. He threw another punch, but the lanky man blocked it and squeezed harder with his other hand. Maurice knew he was a dead man, but he was sure as hell going to make these psychotic shitbags pay the price. He wasn't getting any air and knew he only had a few seconds left.

Maurice thrust his knee up and slammed it into *John*'s groin; he let out a howl and curled his legs up, forcing Maurice upwards and he took the opportunity to pull back and lay a blow to the writhing man's nose. He heard a loud crunch and blood poured from the nostril-holes in the mask, painting the chalky white latex red. *John* went slack and his hand released Maurice's throat. He fell limply to the floor. He rolled off the unconscious man toward the overturned table, came up on one knee, and prepared for the other nut-house rejects to attack.

The big man and much smaller woman stared down at their incapacitated leader and froze. Maurice could feel the adrenaline kick in. He could feel his heartbeat speed up but his mind grew clear. He saw things in slow motion. It had been a long time since he'd felt that way. He'd missed it. He scanned the room and saw the body of the guy wearing the *George Harrison* mask. Blood covered him and the floor around him. Then he saw the shotgun lying in a pool of crimson, and he knew he had to get to it.

It was obvious that the two leather-clad murderers saw his intentions. They stared at Maurice and tensed. Maurice glowered back at them, then at the gun.

One . . . two . . . THREE, he dove for the shotgun. They jumped toward him. A loud crashing noise came from behind Maurice and it forced the two assailants to pause. Maurice's hand found purchase on the wet shotgun and he rolled backward and into the wall. A loud scream filled the room and all three of them looked for the source.

"God *no . . .* " Maurice uttered and chambered the next round.

22.

"Golden Slumbers"

"Ellen NO!" Maurice shouted. She had flung the cooler door open, saw the carnage, and freaked out. She snatched a bottle of Jameson whiskey from the bar, shattered the bottom of it and ran hell-bent-for-leather behind the bar, toward the exit. She didn't have a snowballs' chance in hell, Maurice thought and tears continued to blur his vision.

"I'll get the bitch! You tend to *Jules Winfield,* here," *Paul* ordered and sheathed her shotgun. She pulled out her machete and headed on an intercept course toward the end of the bar.

"On it, luv," *Ringo* said, slapping the flat of the machete's blade against his gloved palm. His large frame cast a long, wide shadow over Maurice and he prepared for the worst. The big man slowly approached him and he raised the shotgun and stood up.

"Back the fuck up Magilla Gorilla," Maurice said. "One more step and you'll be fixin' a hole of your own."

"No need for violence now, mates." *Ringo* side-stepped toward the upright pool table. "We just had some rubbish we had to remove."

"Keep flapping your gums big man and your face is going to look like some of your goddamn bangers and mash." Maurice slowly stepped forward toward the big man, who was now leaning against the pool table.

"Well, the way I see it, you have the gun, so what can this lil' blade do to you?" The big man continued to slap the blade against his palm.

"You're not as dumb as you look, *Ringo*," Maurice said, keeping his aim on his attacker's chest.

A piercing scream broke Maurice's focus and he spun to see the lady dressed as *Paul McCartney* yank Ellen down to the ground by her long black hair- It was a move he never should have made.

Maurice found himself on the ground with the shotgun he'd just had in his hands pointed at him. He swallowed hard and glared up at the behemoth standing over him. He whispered the Lord's Prayer and shot the big man a defiant stare. He had lost everything this vile night, but the last thing he would give up was his pride.

"Shoot me you big shitbag. What are ya waiting for? Permission? You big pussy," Maurice spat. He heard Ellen's cries and the sound of struggle, but realized he had his own death to deal with. He lifted his chin as *Ringo* tucked the cold barrel under it and pushed it up. "What? You have to have a woman tell you what to do?" He knew it was a gamble, but it was all he had.

"Shut the hell up," *Ringo* shouted.

The sounds of a vicious struggle behind him caused Maurice to jump underneath the aim of the big man's shotgun. A slight movement from behind the pool table caught his attention and he tried to calm his breathing. There seemed to be one last hope in this cesspool of sorrow.

"I'm going to end this, right here and now, say good night, *Gracie*," The big man leaned down and shoved the heavy 12 gauge into Maurice's throat.

Ringo suddenly stood up straight, dropped his massive arms and let the gun clank to the floor. His masked face stared straight ahead at the bar. He looked like a marionette as Maurice looked on. The big man collapsed to his knees as Daddy pulled the long blade of his Bowie knife away. The fresh, dark red blood caught the glint of the Christmas lights in its reflection and he, too, fell in a heap on the floor of the bloody bar.

Maurice crawled over to Daddy and grabbed his limp arm. He rolled him over. "Hang in there, we're gonna be okay," he said, but he could tell by Daddy's chalky white skin color that he'd lost too much blood. But he saved his life. He felt the tears come again, but this time they were in shame for judging the man and all of Ashley's family. *No time for that shit*, he thought and caught Daddy forcing a weak smile. Daddy motioned with a weak wave for him to come closer. Maurice leaned in and put his ear to the dying man's mouth. Daddy grabbed his hand, held it tight, and pulled him in close.

"Run dumb ass . . . "

Daddy smiled and Maurice caught a tear running down the burly man's bearded jowls. He looked back and saw *Paul* put a bullet in Ellen's head. He knew he had to go, and he did.

It wasn't until he busted through the blue tarp and scaled down the deck into the waist-deep snow that he realized just how fucked up he was. Blood was pouring out if his side from the bullet. While it didn't penetrate, it still hurt like a sonofabitch and blood ran from that wound as he sprinted, as quickly as he could manage, for his life. As much as his blood flowed from his body, it paled in comparison to the tears of pain and loss he shed with each labored step he took into the thick woods outside the Torchlight Inn. The storm raged on all around him as he staggered, and he made it a good twenty yards before the adrenaline wore off and he collapsed into a deep snow bank.

As the blood loss and fatigue overtook him, he could smell the bitterness of propane and burning wood. His tears never stopped as his eyes were filled with darkness.

His heart wept.

23.

"Carry that weight"

Maurice could barely breathe. The gaping slash in his side sent torrents of shooting pain through his entire torso. It was made worse with every breath he attempted. The flesh wound in his left thigh stung as if a million pissed off wasps had used it for target practice. His vision was blurred and he couldn't feel much of his body. The smell of blood and burning wood filled his crusted nostrils. He didn't know how long he lay there, buried in the deep snow. All he could hear was the sizzling and cracking of a nearby fire and that of the crows cawing high above him in amongst the tall pines and white birch trees.

"The bar," he panicked as he realized the source of the smoky smells and cracking sounds. His heart raced and tried to sit up. The snow covering him was heavy and wet. At least the bleeding had stopped. He managed to dig himself out of the snowdrift. Every part of his body shot with pain from the many small cuts, bruises and burns. He caught a whiff of burnt hair and flailed his hands about his head. He groped at his hair and found a huge patch in the back was burned clean to the scalp. The skin was blistered and he could feel a sticky liquid oozing from them. As he felt down his back, while struggling to stand, he found that the rear of his jacket was burned through as well.

"God damn," he croaked.

The sky was calling for twilight and he could see the long path that led through the woods back to the bar. Not that he had to look that hard considering the deep red blood trail that splattered the white snow through the naked trees. He focused his eyes in the weak light and tried to remember what the hell had happened. He stumbled forward through the deep snow, following the path.

Dark plumes of black smoke and ash filled the sky directly at the end of the path. He cried with every step he took. It felt like a million small razor blades had made a cross-hatch pattern over every inch of his beating body. His heart sank as the thought of Ashley hit him like a ten-pound sledgehammer. He hoped that maybe his eyes were playing tricks on him. Maybe it was all a big horrible practical joke or an alcohol induced nightmare. Anything but what his heart spoke to him and his head agreed. He picked up his pace, ignoring sharp and agonizing pangs of pain, and made his way down the dimly lit path.

He followed the bloody path; realized, as his head began to spin, that it was his own blood that he was following. His stomach began to churn and he felt bile begin to burn all the way up his oesophagus and into the back of his throat.

He tripped as he left the woods and fell onto the volleyball courts that, in the summertime, were filled with drunken participants. But now the courts were covered in deep snowdrifts and pieces of burning timber and smoldering ash. He caught his balance and stared out across the parking lot of the burning bar. It looked like black wrinkled fingers jutting out from the snow-covered earth. Large tendrils of smoke and flames leapt high into the gray morning sky as if praying to the almighty for acceptance and begging for entrance to the heavenly resting place.

The Torchlight Inn was no more, just a charred black skeleton that belied the massacre that had occurred inside just a few hours before. The makeshift deck lay in a burning pile and he could make out bits and pieces of bodies and limbs. They, too, seemed to be reaching out to heaven. The only thing left standing was the metal cooler. It was charred black and stood all alone. Its dark form appeared be in mourning as it stood in sad contrast with the slowly lightening sky.

He broke free from the fire's hypnotic trance and jerked his head about, looking for Ashley. The parking lot was filled with snow. Ash covered cars, and he heard the roar of an engine and the blaring of music coming from the front of the burning bar. He shambled as fast as he could through the almost thigh-deep snow and the sheer pain racking his body.

He stepped through the snow and over burnt bodies, large chunks of timbers and pieces of the bar. As he rounded what was left of the entrance to the bar, he saw a large white SUV fishtail in the slick snow and head south down the road. He could have sworn he heard the sound of *"Good Morning, Good Morning"* coming from the vehicle as it sped away.

"What the fuck…" he started, but was interrupted by movement off to his right. From the flagpole in front of the remains of the bar. He stopped breathing. He had to squint to keep the morning sun's rays from blinding him as he tried to see what was dangling from the tall flagpole. The brutal Lake Ontario winds whipped across the open parking lot and sent a whitewash of snow as tall as the flagpole to cover the entire area. He covered his head and cringed in pain as the cold burned his charred and blistered skin. He staggered closer to the object bouncing against the pole and stared up.

Maurice examined the thing strapped to the pole as it swayed in the strong winter breeze and his heart felt as if it would explode into a million fleshy shards as his mind tried to wrap around just what he was looking at. Once he realized what it was, he wished he had died back in the frozen snow bank of the woods.

There, swaying in the early morning light and in time with the Arctic-like winds was a body. Or what was *left* of a body. It had no arms or legs. Just a blood-soaked torso that was tied with nylon rope to the pole like a disgraced sailor to his ship's mast. Although this was no sailor.

It was Ashley.

Her arms and legs had been crudely hacked off, the bloody stumps cauterized. He stared in disbelief and horror as tears gushed from his wide eyes. He felt his knees shake and he let out a loud, baleful cry that sent the crows scattering from their woodland perches.

Her once brilliant brown eyes stared into nothingness, her mouth hung wide open, and Maurice could see that most of her teeth had been shattered or pulled out. Her once soft, alabaster skin was now the color of crimson covering yellow and blue brutalized flesh. He wanted to stop looking but found himself unable to turn away, even though his soul was shattered more and more with each new gruesome detail discovered.

The cruel wind continued to batter Maurice's exposed skin but he didn't feel anything but anger, sorrow and loss. The tears that fled his eyes froze on his frostbitten cheeks as they made their escape. He wiped his eyes and saw something sticking out of her jacket pocket. He shook as he stepped closer and reached for her. He had to stop her body from swaying in order to reach the pocket. The touch of her broke him. His temples throbbed and he grit his teeth. His vision flashed white and he let out a primal scream again that broke through the howling winds. It was at that moment his shaking hand found purchase on the object sticking out of her torn and burnt jacket pocket. He pulled it out and staggered backward wiping more tears from his eyes as he examined the object in his quivering hands.

It was a book.

The sound of numerous sirens filled the morning air and he didn't even notice. He just stared, a frozen glare, at the book.

The torn cover read:

"The Catcher in the Rye". He was dumbfounded. *Why?* was all he could muster. He noticed a bookmark jutting out from inside the book. The winds picked up and nearly yanked the book and the bookmark out of his numb hands. He held fast to them both and examined the folded up piece of paper.

It was a birth certificate, along with a picture of Ashley. On the birth certificate, it read:

Julia Rita Chapman.

Ashley's mutilated corpse swung like a pendulum in the harsh winter morning winds as the fire trucks and Wayne County Sheriff cars pulled into the smoldering remnants of the Torchlight Inn's parking lot.

Maurice collapsed into a heap in the deep, cold snow. He dropped the book and the worn piece of paper. The wind seized the bloodstained document and whisked it away southward.

He cried out and buried his head into the ash-covered snow.

Epilogue

"A day in the life"

"Well that was a mighty fine night, if I say so meself," *Paul* quipped as she yanked off her blood-covered mask and chucked it into the large Wal-Mart bag sitting between her feet in the back-seat of the speeding SUV.

"Aye, that it was, my dear," *John* stated. His voice was cold and monotone. He held the blood-soaked bandage on his nose and swallowed a bit of blood.

"Check it off the list," he ordered and stared straight ahead at the snow-covered road. The final chords of "*Across the Universe*" faded.

The redhead took the pen from her inside shirt pocket, perused the large binder on her lap, and proceeded to check off the section entitled: *Lennon*. She flipped the pages over and rubbed her freckled chin. She fumbled with the pages and finally came to rest on one section and smirked.

"What's next?" *John* asked as he removed his sweat-soaked mask in one quick movement and threw it to the redhead in the back seat.

She shoved the masks into the bag, cinched it up, and chucked it in the back. She went back to the large binder and chortled aloud.

"Ah, yes. Very fitting I must say." The redhead smiled as she looked over the large binder on her lap. She paused, pulled a CD from one of the binder's pages and handed it to the large man in the passenger seat. He accepted it and slid it into the CD player.

She placed the binder on the empty seat next to her, reached into the back of the SUV, and pulled out a box with the words *Jones* written in black Sharpie maker.

She opened the box and her eyes grew wide with excitement.

"Hope you have your passports in order boys, we are headed home." She laughed and handed the big man his new mask.

"Me? For Christ's sake, why do I always get stuck being the drummer?" the large man pouted as he stared at the gaunt *Charlie Watts* mask. He gripped his bandaged midsection and pain shot through his large frame. However, the promise of more carnage was better than any painkiller known to man.

The white SUV turned onto the New York State Thruway, headed east towards New York City, and disappeared into the snowstorm as the haunting tones of *"Sympathy for the devil"* wafted on the cold wintry breeze.

BONUS STORY

August 16, 1977
(The Death and Birth of The King)

Make the world go away

The young boy sat cross-legged on his cramped bedroom floor with a happy smile on his distorted face. A defect of birth left him with an abnormally pronounced cleft pallet and his left eye extruded enough that it seemed like it would pop out at any given moment and bounce off his blotchy cheek. The small room walls splattered with posters of The Beatles, The Rolling Stones, and Buddy Holly and all other manner of rock n' roll royalty. However, the most precious, moldy real estate was reserved for his favorite, The *King*. The comfort of the soft scratching of the needle on the soothing vinyl record filled his happy ears. Elvis crooned, lamenting the dark life of living in the ghetto.

He sat surrounded by stacks of record albums, high enough that they almost touched the yellowing ceiling. The colorful albums created castle walls of vinyl and he was king within the sonic sanctuary. Inside the only things, his long dead mother left him, her massive record collection and his best friend, the *Stereophonic Music Master-1000* record player. They offered sweet sounds and audible promises of a better place where he wasn't different and laughter was because of true happiness, not his dreaded deformities. Elvis and the Beatles offered him an endless ticket on a bus to a world where he wasn't considered a monster when he went outside. That was *if* his Father allowed him to go outside. He knew the old drunk was embarrassed of him. He could live with that. What he was growing increasingly intolerant of was his ignorant Father's hatred for the only that mattered to the young boy.

His love for music.

The old man never understood his *"monster-son's obsession with his bitch of a mother's music,* and his hatred for it all seeped incessantly from the old man's beer soaked pores. The bitter old man constantly tried to toss the young boy's records into the dumpster behind their dilapidated tenement. The young boy had kept the stinky bastard at bay so far. He worried daily that there would come a time where he wouldn't be able to stop the vile attempts. His large head throbbed with anger and his taught limbs twitched with anxiety at the thought.

Over my dead body, the young boy repeated under his breath for hours until he eventually fell asleep to the low tones of his own determined mantra. But today was a good day. The crotchety old man was a few blocks away at a bar; watching a Red Sox double header with his alcoholic, slack jawed beer buddies. That meant the young boy could sit in his room, drink his grape Kool-Aid and raise the drawbridge to his cardboard and vinyl castle and lose himself in a symphonic euphoria.

The record collection was meticulously organized and he knew it by heart.

What will it be today Mom? He asked into the thick air, fingering the collection and walking the perimeter of the room, sipping from his large plastic mug. The magical *Stereophonic- Music Master-1000* blasted *Mother's Little Helper* as he continued his search for his next sonic salvation. He had no idea what time it was. The "E" section of the record collection blocked the only window, blotting out the light with it. He never cared much for time anyway. The ticks on the clock to a young boy essentially locked in his own bedroom didn't hold a lot of merit. He measured time in the length of 45s and 78's. Those records were all that mattered to him.

He walked the square of music, waiting for its usual *Voice* to speak to him. Waiting for musical inspiration. He'd grown close to the soothing *Voice* that made his life bearable and, combined with the record collection and the record player; the ever-present *Voice* completed his entire circle of friends. He grew more anxious and distraught as he walked while with the *Voice* was silent. His heart began to skip beats and sweat began to pour down his face. The *Voice* had never let him down. It had always kept him company. Had always told him what to listen to. There was a time he thought it was his dead mother but once he started reading the Bible and accepted Jesus on the throne of his heart, he realized that it would be painfully difficult for her to speak to him will being drawn and quartered in the fiery pits of Hell. Suicide was a sin, while he loved his mother he knew it wasn't her and that left him wondering the true source of the *Voice.*

The deafening silence of the missing Voice stole his breath. A bit of afternoon sun splintered underneath the bedroom door and the only sound in the dark room was the hiss and repetitive thump of the tone arm on the record player, waiting impatiently for its next selection.

"Oh my dear friend. Where did you go? Tell me. Please tell me what to play next," The young boy pleaded, draining the remainder of his drink.

"*Danny Boy,*" The usually soothing *Voice* shouted into the young boy's mind. He fell to the matted and stained shag-carpeted floor, dropping the cup and staring wide-eyed.

"*Danny Boy,*" the *Voice* kept repeating. The young boy jumped to his feet and ran to the exact spot where the album sat, jutting out bizarrely an inch beyond all the other records on the makeshift shelves. Waiting.

The young boy pulled the record from its jacket and placed it on the record player. He carefully placed the Stone's album back in its jacket and put it back in its correct spot on the shelf. The *King* began to sing sweetly of Danny Boy and the calling pipes. It felt good. It felt right to the young boy. He watched the vinyl spin around and closed his eyes, lost in the lilting chorus and tears surprised him as they raced down his clammy face.

An ear-splitting screech from the record needle filled the room and dropped him to his knees. The music died with it. The song stopped in mid-chorus, leaving only a painful ringing in his ears. What light was breaking underneath the door was blacked out as the young man's body and soul jolted with unbelievable pain and sorrow.

It took a few pain-filled moments for him to shake his clear. The *Voice* was mumbling, but he couldn't make out the jumbled words. He got to his feet. His knees shook like leaves on a tree but managed to keep his balance. The *Voice* was distant and speaking one word.

Murdered!

Murdered!

Murdered!

The word bore into his temples. He felt the word pulse through his defective body. It wouldn't be denied.

The *Voice* suddenly fell silent as a pounding came at the door.

The door kicked open and the young boy's Father staggered into the doorway. A large bottle of Vodka hung slack in one hand, in the other a burning cigarette.

"Well, well Mama's boy, I got sum news fer ya," The slurring was hard to decipher but the young boy had gotten proficient in drunken-ese.

The young boy recoiled against the far wall of records, spreading his arms out, covering them.

"Yer gonna love this ya lil' tittie baby," The Father pointed at his startled son.

"Leave mm-me alone," The young boy's voice came out garbled and weak.

"Shut the hell up ya little freak. This is *my* house and I'm tired of takn' cer' of yer sorry ass. You gonna love to hear that yer prec'us *King*, Elvis is fuckin' *dead*! How ya feel 'bout that huh?" His Father staggered like a zombie into the bedroom, grabbing the record shelf to balance himself. He chortled and took a swig from the bottle and let the brown liquid pour down the front of his already stained, white t-shirt.

"Wha...what? NO!" The young boy's mumble exploded into a shriek.

"Oh, you bet your sorry little ass. The piece shit, popped too many pills 'n they found 'em dead as a door nail on the shitter. All hail the mighty *King*," The drunk laughed and grabbed the record shelf and pulled it down, sending the entire wall of vinyl crashing onto the floor.

"STOP!" The young boy screeched.

'I'm tired of all this shit music n' all this...this hero worship shit, I am gonna smash these fuckin' records. It done didn't stop yer whore of a mother from killin' herself and I'm done had it with yer shit too! There ALL fuckin' outta here ya hear me boy?" The Father said and started to stomp on all the records, now spread out in the floor.

"Papa, NO!" The young boy leapt down on top of the shattered vinyl.

The Father yanked the young boy back by his long brown hair, tossed him against the right wall-causing the shelves to cave under the attack, and sent its contents spilling onto the floor. Joining the other crushed remnants of his mother's precious collection.

The young boy's hysterical torrent of tears soaked the once beautiful artwork of Janis Joplin's *Pearl*. When he rolled over, whole chunks of soggy, colorful cardboard came up with his cheek. He stared up at his lilting Father with a burning hatred that filled every inch of his frail body.

"Now, don't ya look 'et me like that, ya lil' shit. Stop yer damn cryin' ya big pussy. I'm gonna give ya som'n to cry about!" The Father kicked his sprawled son in the ribs and stepped over him to assault the final wall of useless records. He tripped over the *Stereophonic Music Master-1000,* causing him to drop his bottle.

"Motherfucker!" he caught his balance and stared down and the silent record player. "Goddamn tired of this piesh a shhhit blaring that shit all hoursss u the damn, nigh," He stomped down with all his weight with the steel-toed *Wolverine* work boot and made short work of the old tone arm cobra. Dozens of pieces of plastic, metal and vinyl filled the air and the young boy tried to stop his drunken old man but his body refused his respond.

The Father stared down at the young boy and jerked back in a belly laugh. Then he caught himself from falling and remembered his Fatherly job wasn't yet complete. He spit a huge snot-filled gob onto what remained of the record player and smiled. He fell into the last shelf and pulled out the Beatles's Sgt. *Pepper's Lonely Hearts Club Band*, shot his frozen son a look of disdain and disgust, and held it out for him to see.

"See, thessse damn hippies and stonrs are pure evil ya dum sumbitch," He looked at the cover and shook his sweat-covered face. "Goddamn garbage n' ya can bet yer boney little ass that these losers'll prolly join that fat ass Presley in Hell befur to lung. Ya can bet yer messsh'd up fachhe" He knelt down, pulling the record from its sleeve and smiled wide. His yellow and black teeth smelled as bad as they looked.

"This shit right her isssh the damn reason yer Mama put a bullet into her damn brainpan. Brainwashin' bullshit from fake ass rich bassstards, that just smoke refer, snort cocaine n shoot all that oth'r shit," The young boy jerked his head away from his teetering Father.

*Don't let him get away with this Graham. Irreprehensible, jealous sycophants like your Father are responsible for my death as well as many others. You **MUST** stop him!* The Voice returned with a deafening blast. It startled the young man, for it never had used his name before.

"Don't turn away from me boy. Ya gotta see this. I'm a gonna make a damn man outta ya, even if it kills me," The Father smashed the record over his son's head and laughed. He fell down on one knee, still laughing, holding the shards of the album in his hand.

It is time to act Graham. Stop his abuse. The Voice commanded and the young boy felt the words in his heart. They felt...True and righteous.

"Guess I'm gonna have to just start usin' my fists on ya boy, once I done with all these goddamn' records," The Father's laughter echoed inside the destroyed castle walls as he stood up and loomed over his prone son.

"But first, I need to drain the main vain. Ya don't mind do ya boy?" The Father unzipped his dirty work pants and yanked his pecker out and a golden flow of piss arced out and onto the pile of smashed records. The old man laughed and bounced up and down, turning it into a game as he tried to find an Elvis album. His mocking laughter echoed louder as he located the King's Christmas record.

"Hot damn, that wass, yer Mama's favorite. This one's fer you Peggy Sue," Urine splattered on the young face of Elvis, soaking it through. The old man ran out of piss and zipped up and turned for the door.

"Ya better have all thisss sshit, picked up by the time I get back. If ya don't, ya might wanna go look fer yer bitch of a mamma's gun," The Father laughed again...kicked the young boy in the thigh and stumbled out the door.

The only light was coming from the kitchen windows, where the old man was headed for a cold beer.

Anger sprang through Graham and he felt as if he were about to explode. He felt a renewed strength overtake him. Every muscle in his thin body tightened. It felt like a thousand volts were pulsing through him and the Voice urged him on.

It ends today Graham. It ends NOW.

Graham's once trembling hand, now filled with vibrant energy snatched up the bottle of whiskey and he leapt to his feet. He had never felt this invigorated or so...alive. He liked it. He loved it.

The Voice was right. It ALL ends NOW!

DO IT!

He bolted toward the old man, hunched over inside the fridge. The drunk must have heard the floor creak, because he turned around in time to see the Mr. Boston bottle coming crashing down upon his head.

Shards of glass sliced into the Father's forehead and one large piece popped his left eye like a ripe tomato. He fell to the cold floor in a heap.

"Wha...wha... the fuc, I kill ya...bas..."The Father grabbed at his eye as a ribbon of blood flowed from it.

End it Graham. End it now... my Avenger!" The Voice rang in the young boy's mind.

"You will never hurt anyone ever again," Graham held the jagged neck of the bottle in his blood slathered hand. With one wide eye, and a deformed smile, he spent the next nine hours slicing and dissecting his Father. Whom he let linger on the doorway to death just so his Father could fully experience the pain that he'd put him through for all these dark and sorrow filled ten years. A thick layer of blood caked and coagulated in the grain of the old wooden floor and the room smelled of copper, feces, and freedom.

Graham stood up and stared down and the butchered remains of what used to be his biological Father. He smiled, slipped in the gore as he pulled the pitcher of grape kool-Aid out of the open fridge and took a long swig. He dropped the empty Tupperware container onto what he only could assume was his Father's liver. But he couldn't be sure. It was the biggest organ inside the diabolical man's body after all.

You've done well Graham. But we have much work to do. This is just but the beginning of many wrongs that you must right. Are you ready? Are you ready my avenger? Are you ready my son? The Voice beamed inside Graham's mind and it made him smile.

"I will never again let any injustice go unpunished. On this, I swear!" Graham shouted into the dark apartment. Sharp shadows cradled the horrific scene as he headed to his bedroom and packed some clothes, a few cassettes and a Halloween *John Lennon* mask his mother had bought for him last year.

Good my Avenger... Now that you are ready, let us begin.

"What now? What's next?" Graham asked. With a big backpack over his shoulder and holding his Father's pistol he found under his parent's bed.

Graceland. The Voice commanded.

And the Voice would be Graham's constant companion for the rest of his days.

Thomas A. Erb is a genre fiction writer exploring all shades of darkness and light and the varying definitions of heroism. Refusing to pigeonhole his writing, Thomas continues to craft tales that blur the lines of dark, fantasy, thriller, weird western, science fiction for both adult and young adult audiences.

A member of the HWA, Thomas is also an artist/illustrator of murals and comic book/graphic novels.

When not writing, Thomas enjoys quality films, television shows, role-playing games, playing drums, comic books and rooting for the Dallas Cowboys and New York Yankees. He lives in upstate New York with his wife Michelle and their old crotchety yellow lab, Rask.

WWW.CROWDEDQUARANTINE.CO.UK